EDEN COLLEGE

ELLA AT EDEN

For my two favourite things to come out of the UK—my mum and dad.

Scholastic Australia
An imprint of Scholastic Australia Pty Limited
PO Box 579 Gosford NSW 2250
ABN 11 000 614 577
www.scholastic.com.au

Part of the Scholastic Group
Sydney • Auckland • New York • Toronto • London • Mexico City
• New Delhi • Hong Kong • Buenos Aires • Puerto Rico

Published by Scholastic Australia in 2021.

Cover and internal illustrations by Danielle McDonald.

NATIONAL LIBRARY OF AUSTRALIA
A catalogue record for this book is available from the National Library of Australia

ISBN: 978-1-76112-335-1

Typeset in Carniola

Printed in China by Hang Tai Printing Company Limited.
This product is made of material from well-managed FSC®-certified forests, recycled materials, and other controlled sources.

FSC www.fsc.org MIX Paper | Supporting responsible forestry FSC® C023121

10 9 8 7 6 5 4 3 2 25 26 27 28 / 2

EDEN COLLEGE

ELLA AT EDEN

The London Thief

LAURA SIEVEKING

A Scholastic Australia book

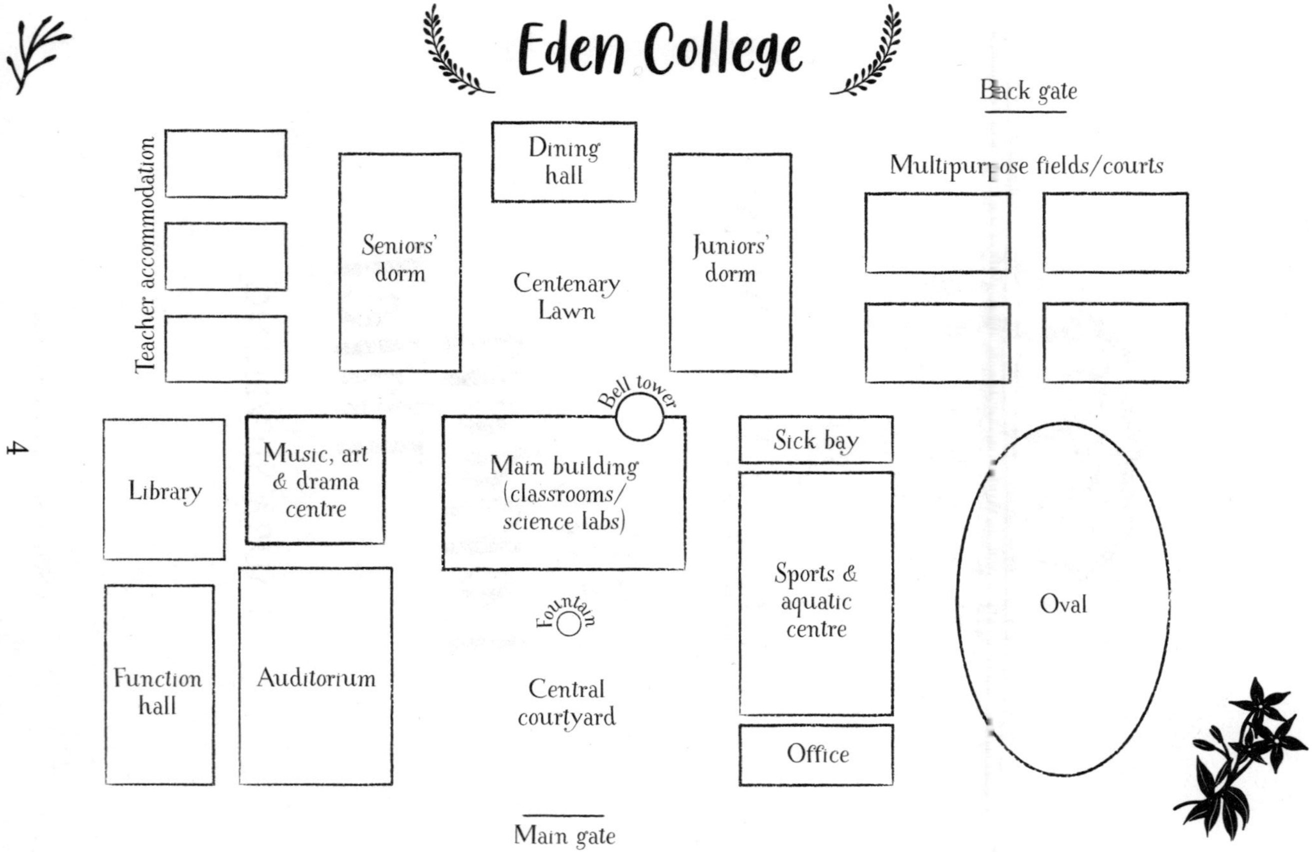
Eden College
Back gate
Teacher accommodation
Seniors' dorm
Dining hall
Centenary Lawn
Juniors' dorm
Multipurpose fields/courts
Bell tower
Library
Music, art & drama centre
Main building (classrooms/ science labs)
Sick bay
Function hall
Auditorium
Fountain
Central courtyard
Sports & aquatic centre
Oval
Office
Main gate

Juniors' Dorm

Level 1 (ground)

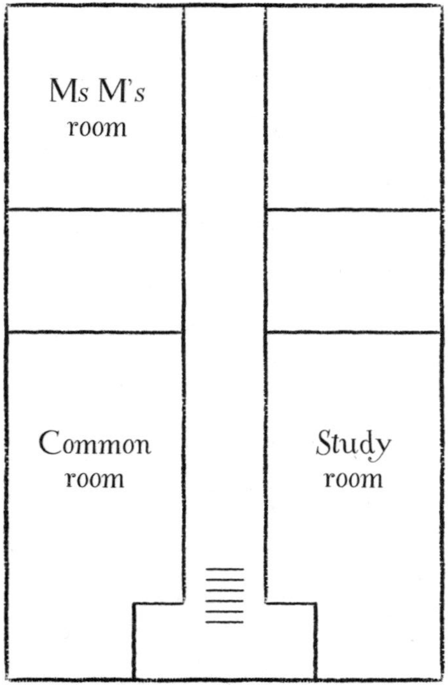

Level 2

Year 7 rooms

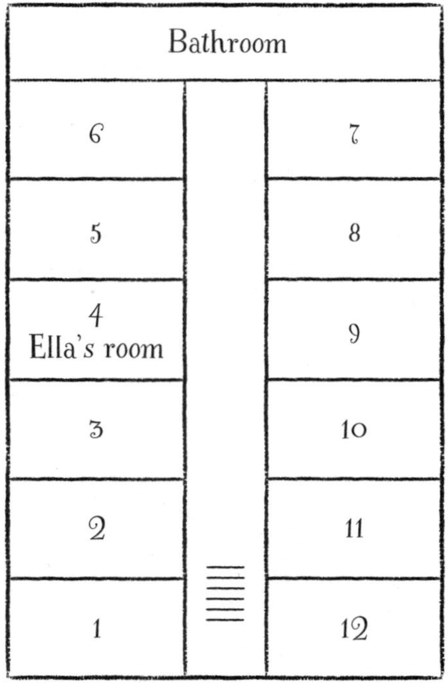

Chapter 1

The smell of the hot winter's lunch enveloped me as I entered the dining hall. I loved the winter lunch options, as there was always some sort of warm food to have, like pasta, casserole or soup. I joined the end of the line, and craned my head to see what was on offer today. Along with the usual selection of wraps and sandwiches, I could see piles of small aluminium foil trays with cardboard lids. One stack had a sign saying, 'Pasta Bolognese'. Another said, 'Vegetarian fried rice'. When I got to the front of the line, I selected a tray of pasta Bolognese and took a disposable bamboo fork, a few serviettes and an orange juice box from the end of the serving area.

'Where should we eat today?' I asked my three best friends, who had just collected their own lunches. We looked around the dining hall, which was already quite full and noisy. Usually, we would take our lunch outside to eat on one of the lawns, but it was a particularly cold and windy day.

'Let's go to the break room,' Zoe suggested.

Violet, Grace and I nodded in agreement, and started towards the big doors that led out of the dining hall into the school grounds.

'Stop right there, girls,' said a stern voice.

We froze and looked back at the vice headmistress, wondering which one of us had committed a misdemeanour (which is a fancy way of saying done something wrong).

'Grace, look at your leg,' Ms Montgomery said. Her brow was furrowed and her eyes were piercing.

We all looked at Grace's leg and saw her stockings had a giant hole in them, revealing a big patch of her bare skin underneath.

'Oh, oops! I must have snagged them this morning!' Grace said airily.

'Well, it's not good enough. Eden College girls are ladies, and ladies do not walk around with holes in their stockings! You need to go back to the dormitory before the end of lunch and change,' Ms Montgomery snapped.

Grace nodded and we all bundled out of the dining hall doors into the cold winter air.

'I don't think I have any stockings left that *don't* have holes,' Grace said miserably.

'Just go up to the dorm and take a pair from my drawer after you finish your lunch,' Zoe said kindly. 'I have lots of spares and we are the same size.'

Grace thanked Zoe with a little side hug. 'What would I do without you guys?' she smiled.

Grace was right. What *would* we do without each other? My three best friends also happened to be my roommates here at Eden College, and we were always there for each other. Grace was a scatterbrain, but so brave and she helped us all feel more confident when we were low. Zoe was smart and logical, and could help with any problem, whether troublesome stocking holes or frustrating maths equations. And Violet was kind and supportive, and provided a sense of calm and comfort whenever we were upset or homesick. They really were the best friends anyone could ask for.

We walked up the path as it snaked its way around the manicured gardens of Centenary Lawn. I held my warm food tucked against my chest, with my blazer pulled tight across my body to keep out the blustering winter wind. Even with my shirt, tunic, jumper and blazer on, it was still cold and I couldn't wait to get inside the warmth of the Year 7 break room.

We all picked up the pace into a little jog as that warmth beckoned. Zoe flung open the door to the main building and we bundled inside and down the hall. The Juniors' break room was a place where the Year 7 students could relax and hang out during school hours. There were couches, beanbags and a small station for making cups of tea and hot chocolate.

We walked over to our usual spot, where two couches facing each other stood waiting. The break room heater was on, so I stripped off my blazer and sat down with my lunch. I peeled back the cardboard lid to reveal the delicious-smelling pasta.

Grace took a mouthful of her steaming lunch and dropped a big splodge of Bolognese onto her jumper.

'Oh, man!' she cried.

Violet handed her some napkins while smothering a giggle.

'I can't wait for the art competition announcement after lunch,' Violet said enthusiastically. 'I think you might win, Ella!'

A wave of anticipation and nervousness washed over me. All of Year 7 had entered artworks into a portrait competition for a big upcoming exhibition. The best bit was the winner would join a group of students from other year levels on a trip to London to exhibit their artwork in an international art competition! The thought of flying to London made my stomach flutter with excitement.

'Maybe,' I said. 'There were a lot of good entries.'

I had painted a portrait based on a photo of my Nanna Kate. The only rule for the competition was to create a piece of art based on a person, but we were allowed to use paint, charcoal, pencil or even do a sculpture. I had chosen paint and tried to create as realistic a portrait of Nanna Kate as I could. I was pretty happy with the end result, and by the feedback I'd received from my art teacher, Mrs Hodges, I thought I was in with a pretty good chance.

'Who did you paint, Grace?' I asked, realising I had never seen Grace's entry.

'I painted my brother, Alec, but it's not very realistic,' she said, scrunching up her nose. 'I was reading some stuff about these painters who make really weird-looking art by showing all the different parts of the face on one side, so I thought I'd try it. It makes it look a bit strange, though.'

'Well, it's not a competition for the most realistic piece of art,' I said encouragingly. Even though I wanted to be nice about Grace's art, I knew her work would have been something pretty out there. Just like Grace's personality, she wasn't one to keep to the rules and colour in the lines. Her art was always a bit different to everyone else's, so maybe she was right about not being likely to win. Some of the other artworks I had seen entered were absolutely amazing. One girl, Annabelle, had done a pencil drawing of her mum and it looked so real you could actually see the life in her eyes. She was probably my main competition at the Year 7 level.

'How exciting to go to London, though!' Zoe said, her eyes gleaming. 'I went two summers ago with my family, and it was so cool. We saw a musical in the West End and caught the Tube everywhere.'

'What's the Tube?' I asked.

'It's the underground train system in London.'

'Are you talking about London?' a voice said from the beanbags behind us. It was Saskia and her friends, Portia and Mercedes.

'Yeah, about the art competition winners getting to go there,' Zoe said.

'I've been to London, like, four times,' Saskia said,

flicking her blonde ponytail over her shoulder. 'I got the funniest photo of me in front of Big Ben. We took it with Big Ben in the distance behind me and angled the camera so it looked like I was holding it on my hand!'

'Who is Big Ben?' I asked.

Saskia cackled, 'Oh, Ella! It's a clock, not a person!' She laughed loudly.

My cheeks felt hot. I'd never been to London. I'd actually never been overseas at all. Girls from Eden College were always going on amazing trips overseas—skiing in France or to see the Grand Canyon in America. My Nanna Kate had travelled all over the world, and I really wanted to do that myself someday. But for now, I didn't think it was likely that my family would take me on such a big trip.

'I've never been to London either,' Grace said.

'But you go to America all the time for your dad's work, right?' Saskia replied.

Grace's eyes flicked towards me. She nodded silently, waving her hand dismissively at the same time.

As if sensing my awkwardness, Zoe patted my knee.

'You'll get your chance,' she whispered.

I smiled gratefully. Zoe had been my best friend for as long as I could remember, and she always knew how I was feeling, even when I didn't say anything.

'I'd better go get my new stockings before lunch ends,' Grace said, getting up. As she stood, a piece of pasta rolled off her dress and onto the floor. 'Oops!' Grace bent down, picked up the spiral and popped it into her mouth.

'Gross, Grace!' Violet said, shaking her head.

Grace shrugged and skipped out of the break room door.

'Have any of you seen Grace's portrait?' I asked.

Zoe and Violet shook their heads.

'She was working on it after school with Mrs Hodges,' Zoe said.

'I don't want to be mean,' I said, 'but it sounded a little weird! What was that about all the parts of the face being on one side? Wouldn't the ears be with the eyes?!'

'Well, you know Grace!' Zoe shrugged.

'What would you do if you *did* win, Ella?' Violet asked. 'Wouldn't you be nervous to go all the way to London?'

Butterflies flitted around my stomach. The thought of travelling overseas without my friends or family filled me with apprehension. *Apprehension* is a fancy word for feeling really nervous. But there was also excitement mixed in.

The bell pierced the air and we gathered up our rubbish and put it into the recycling and waste bins in the corner of the break room. We pulled our blazers back on over our jumpers and Zoe wound her Eden College scarf around her neck. Then we headed through the central courtyard towards the auditorium for the art competition announcement.

To help calm my nerves, I linked arms with Zoe, who gave my elbow a reassuring pat. And as we walked towards the auditorium, I crossed my fingers and hoped.

Chapter 2

We sat in the flip-down seats of the auditorium, with the lights shining down on the stage in front of us. The whole school could fit in the cavernous room, which was alive with chatter. Grace had caught up to us, with her fresh stockings on. My leg jittered nervously next to hers as we awaited the start of the special assembly.

'Hey, Ella,' a voice said from the aisle. It was Lauren, our Year 12 School Captain. 'I saw your portrait. Good luck today—I think you have a real chance!'

'Thanks, Lauren,' I said, smiling. I had gotten to know Lauren quite well in the school musical earlier in the year, when she played the main role of the Snow Queen and I played a woodland dryad. Lauren was always so kind to the girls in the younger years, often giving us advice or just being a friendly face to talk to. She'd become like a big sister to me. That was one of the great things about being in a boarding school—it was like you lived with a few hundred sisters.

Lauren walked down the front and climbed the stairs to take her seat on the stage with Ms Montgomery and the headmistress, Mrs Sinclair. Mrs Hodges was also on stage, because she was the head of the art department and one of the judges of the art competition.

Mrs Sinclair rose to her feet and approached the lectern. 'Good morning, girls.'

'Good morning, Mrs Sinclair,' we all chorused.

'Today is a very special assembly. I know many of you entered our portrait competition and it gives me great pleasure to now reveal the winners. Our winners will be going to London with Mrs Hodges and a team of teachers to stay in a boarding school over there, while exhibiting their artwork in an international, interschool art competition.'

A murmur rose up amongst the students. I bit my lip nervously.

'When I announce the winner for each year group, a picture of their artwork will be displayed on the screen behind me. Then I will invite Mrs Hodges to explain why the panel of judges chose this particular piece,' Mrs Sinclair said, beckoning to Mrs Hodges.

As Mrs Hodges stood up, her skirt billowed about her ankles. I recognised the swirls of yellow, blue and black on her skirt—it was a print of the famous painting, *Starry Night*. Her silver hair was pulled up into a bird's nest of a messy bun and, even from several rows back, I could hear her multiple bangles clacking together as she walked.

'We'll begin with Year 7,' Mrs Sinclair said.

Zoe reached over and held my hand.

'The winner for Year 7 is . . .'

The room was so quiet you could have heard a bubble pop. It was like the entire audience had collectively held its breath as we all leaned forward in our seats.

'Grace!'

Grace?!

I looked up at the screen and saw Grace's artwork for the first time. Underneath was the title, *My Brother, Alec*. As Grace had said, the portrait wasn't a realistic one. There were bright colours spinning all over her brother's face, and exploding from his head were what looked like fireworks or shooting stars. His eyes were large, but there was a softness to them.

Mrs Hodges spoke into the microphone. 'Grace has explored surrealism in her work, which was influenced by famous painters such as Pablo Picasso. In the accompanying description of her painting, she explained that she wanted to show the beautiful difference of her brother Alec's mind. She did this by portraying his thoughts as an explosion of colour, representing his creativity and also his anxiousness. As you can see, Grace's skill and technique are impressive. Grace, please join us on stage.'

Grace stood, her mouth open in shock. She looked at us with wide eyes. Violet let out a little squeal of excitement and Zoe clapped loudly. I sat frozen.

Grace walked up onto the stage and received her certificate from Mrs Sinclair. She was then invited to sit on stage as they moved on to announce the other winners in the other year levels.

I looked down at my hands. My mind was a bundle of confusion. One of my best friends had won. Why wasn't I happy for her? Was I a terrible friend? It was just that I'd worked so hard on my portrait of Nanna Kate, trying to make her as realistic as I could. And yet Grace had won with a painting that was nothing like real life. It didn't seem fair.

The assembly finished and we were dismissed.

'I can't believe Grace is going to London!' Zoe squealed.

Grace came down from the stage and ran towards us. Violet and Zoe enveloped her in their arms in a laughing embrace.

'I can't believe it,' Grace said, holding her hand to her chest. 'I thought my work was too weird to win. I didn't think it was even in with a chance!'

Violet and Zoe stood back from their hug, making room for me to give Grace my own congratulations.

'Well done, Grace,' I said shakily. 'I guess realistic portraits weren't what they were going for.'

Grace's brow momentarily furrowed. She bit her lip.

'I'm sure you'll have an awesome time in London,' I added hastily.

Grace forced a smile.

Zoe frowned as we plunged into an awkward silence.

'Better get to class,' I said, edging my way out of the row of seats and running up the aisle.

I burst out of the auditorium and into the sunny winter's afternoon. I walked quickly up the path, as tears began to prick my eyes. I was embarrassed about crying and began to jog, hoping nobody would see me. But as I entered the main building, I tripped on my undone shoelace and fell to the ground.

'Ella, are you OK? Are you hurt?'

I looked up and saw Lauren, her hand outstretched.

I wiped my eyes. 'No, I'm not hurt,' I said sheepishly. I stood up, feeling a little shaky.

'But you're crying! Do you want me to take you to the school nurse?'

I shook my head, embarrassed. 'I'm not hurt. I'm just being silly about the art competition,' I confessed.

Lauren's eyes softened. 'You really wanted to win, didn't you?'

'I've never been overseas,' I said quietly. 'And Grace's art wasn't even realistic.'

Lauren smiled kindly. 'Ella, art is about conveying emotion, not about looking like a photo. I thought Grace's piece was incredible. And she's one of your best friends. Aren't you happy for her?'

I felt a wash of guilt come over me. Lauren was right. Grace was one of my best friends and I'd been so busy sulking about not winning that I hadn't even hugged her in congratulations. Her art had won fair and square and she deserved to go to London. I sighed sadly. 'You're right. I think I owe her an apology.'

Lauren gave me a little side hug. 'See you later, Ella.'

'Thanks, Lauren,' I said.

I knew exactly where Grace would be—on her way

to her Maths class, which was right next door to mine. I ran ahead of the crowd of students, trying to find her before she went in. Then I saw her long, dark braid from afar and called out to her.

'Grace!'

She spun around and looked surprised to see me.

'Grace, congratulations on your win,' I said breathlessly.

'It's OK, Ella. You don't have to pretend to be happy for me,' she said sadly.

'I *am* happy for you. I'm sorry I didn't say it straight away. I was so busy wallowing in my own disappointment, I overlooked that one of my best friends had just won. Do you forgive me?'

Grace broke into a smile and pulled me into a hug. 'Of course,' she laughed.

One of the best things about Grace was that she never held a grudge. She didn't like fighting and was not one of those girls who would drag on a disagreement for days on end.

'Ella, there you are,' another voice said as I broke

away from my hug with Grace. It was Mrs Sinclair. 'I was looking for you after the assembly, but you disappeared so quickly.'

'Sorry about that,' I said, glancing sheepishly at Grace.

'That's OK. I just had an exciting proposal that I wanted to discuss with you,' she said warmly.

I nodded, listening.

Grace backed away slightly as if to give us privacy, but then bent down and pretended to tie her shoe. I could tell she was trying to hear what Mrs Sinclair was saying, which made me smother a giggle.

'As you know, we have our competition winners going to London for the art exhibit. In your year, Grace is going, as we just announced in the assembly.'

'Yes, she'll be so great,' I said, glancing back at Grace, who was still lingering behind Mrs Sinclair.

'Well, we would like a record of all that happens on the art tour for those of us staying here at Eden, so we are going to be sending a few girls from Eden Press, the school newspaper,' Mrs Sinclair continued.

My heart stopped.

'As Junior Journalist, we'd love to invite you to go.'

My mouth fell open.

'I . . . I . . .' Suddenly, I was completely unable to speak. I had a torrent of feelings rushing around my body, but I couldn't say a single word.

Then a cold realisation hit me: I wasn't sure my parents could afford to pay for a trip like this.

'I'd love to, but I'm not sure my parents . . .' my voice trailed off.

Mrs Sinclair smiled. 'I've already spoken to your parents about this, Ella. They were very keen to give you this opportunity. They also said your Nanna Kate wanted to chip in to help pay for the trip, too. I hear she's quite the adventurer!'

Tears pricked my eyes as I thought of my loving Nanna Kate offering to pay for my ticket to London.

'So, is that a yes?' Mrs Sinclair asked.

'Absolutely! It's a yes, it's a yes!' I blurted.

'WOOOHOOO!' Grace leapt out from behind Mrs Sinclair, clearly startling her, and threw her arms around me in such an energetic way that I toppled backwards to the ground. Suddenly, Grace realised she'd just tackled me to the ground in front of the school's headmistress. She hurriedly pulled me up, and we straightened our skirts and adjusted our blazers.

'Um, sorry about that, Mrs Sinclair!' Grace said with wide eyes.

Mrs Sinclair let out a hearty laugh. 'Am I going to regret sending the pair of you overseas together?' she asked in a jovial voice.

'No, you won't regret it!' Grace and I said in unison.

'Alright, well off to class then, you two,' Mrs Sinclair said, waving us towards our classrooms.

'Yes, of course, let's go, Ella,' Grace said. But as Mrs Sinclair turned to walk away, Grace couldn't help herself and yelled at the top of her lungs, 'London, here we come!'

Chapter 3

Four weeks later.

'Does everyone have their boarding passes?' Mrs Hodges asked, as she bustled around us.

'Yes!' we all chorused excitedly.

I looked around the airport waiting area. We were a large group, with 15 students in total, plus another three teachers. The girls were from a mix of year levels and comprised the winners of the art competition for each grade, plus two runners-up for each of the senior year levels and three Eden Press girls—me, the Year 7

Junior Journalist, Ivy, the Editor from Year 9, and Tilly, the Junior Journalist from Year 8. The other girls I didn't know very well, but I was excited to get to know them better during our stay in London.

'Wait. Where's my boarding pass?' Grace cried, spinning around and squatting down next to her carry-on bag.

'You mean this one?' I asked, plucking at the ticket that was sticking out of her back pocket.

'I'm so glad you are coming,' Grace laughed.

'You'd get lost in the Tower of London without me!' I joked.

'Attention, customers on flight QF198 to Singapore. We are now ready for boarding,' a lilting voice said over the loudspeaker.

Suddenly, a rush of nerves flowed through my body. I was about to board my first ever international flight. We would fly to Singapore, where we would have a stopover, before flying on to London. I'd never been so far from home in my entire life. It was exhilarating, but also terrifying.

'Girls, please bring your carry-on bags and line up over here so I can check each of you off my list as you board the plane,' Mrs Hodges called.

We formed a line and Mrs Hodges checked our names off as the airline stewards scanned our boarding passes. When my turn came, I handed my ticket to the kindly steward, who noticed my trembling hand.

'First time on a plane?' he asked, as he waved my boarding pass over the scanner until it beeped.

'No, but it's my first time overseas,' I whispered.

'You'll love it,' he said, smiling at me. 'Have a good flight, Miss.'

I took a deep breath in and entered the mouth of the closed walkway leading to the plane. When I got to the plane door, a flight attendant checked my boarding pass and directed me to my seat. I smiled when I saw I had a window seat.

'Aw, man, centre seat!' Grace whined, as she glanced between her ticket and the seat numbers.

'At least you are next to me!' I said.

I slid into my seat and tucked my backpack under

the seat in front of me. Gazing out the window, I could see the airport staff loading the luggage into the bowels of the plane. I hoped my bag wouldn't get lost.

'How are they getting your artwork over to London for the competition?' I asked, suddenly realising I hadn't seen any of the winning entries with our luggage.

'Oh, they couriered it all over there a couple of weeks ago. It should be in the gallery already,' Grace said.

I couldn't believe it. Grace's artwork was going to be hanging in a *real* art gallery. In London! Since it was an international competition, our Eden College artwork plus entries from high schools all over the United Kingdom would make up the exhibit. They would all be on display for a week, and then real artists and art critics were going to judge the competition and declare a winner.

'I wonder what the school we are staying at is like,' Grace said. 'I hope it's like Hogwarts!'

I laughed. 'I doubt it, Grace. It's just a normal boarding school, like Eden College.'

'Yeah, but it's in *London*, Ella. Everything is posh and

fancy in London. The Queen lives there, you know.'

I couldn't wait to see all the sights of London. We were going to visit Buckingham Palace, ride the London Eye, which is like a gigantic Ferris wheel that takes you so high up you can overlook the whole city, and even see a musical in the famous West End!

'Please prepare for take-off,' a voice crackled over the loudspeaker.

I squeezed Grace's hand as the flight attendants went through the safety demonstration and did their final checks to make sure everyone's seatbelt was on and carry-on bags stowed. The plane gently chugged along, then paused after it turned onto the long runway. Suddenly, the plane launched itself forward, gathering speed as we took our run-up for take-off.

'Grace, I'm so nervous!' I breathed.

The plane began to lift, and my stomach did a little flip as I felt us pull up off the ground. My ears made a funny popping sound as we climbed higher and higher into the air. Grace handed me some gum to chew, which she said would help with my ears.

Once the plane had reached its cruising altitude, which was just the airline's way of saying flying height, it levelled off so we were straight again and seemed to relax into a smooth, constant speed. There was a quiet *bing* as the seatbelt signs were turned off, meaning we were allowed to move around the plane to go to the toilet if we needed to.

'Ah, smooth sailing now. Are we nearly there?' Grace asked.

'Grace! We've been flying for five minutes! The flight time to Singapore is eight hours! And then we fly another 13 or 14 hours to London!' I said, exasperated.

'Wait, *what?*'

I nodded.

'That's, like, a whole day and night on a plane,' Grace said, scrunching up her nose.

I nodded again.

Grace paused. 'So . . .'

I raised my eyebrows questioningly.

'Noughts and crosses?' she asked.

I laughed.

I stirred in my seat. My neck felt stiff and sore. I pulled my eye mask off and looked around. The plane cabin was dim. Grace breathed heavily as she slept upright in her seat, her head bobbing forward every now and then, which startled her into near consciousness before she settled back into a light sleep.

I pulled open the window shutter next to me and looked outside. It was pitch black. The only light I could see was the one blinking on the wing of the plane. I tried to look downwards to see if I could see anything, but the sky just fell away into blackness.

I swivelled and kneeled up on my seat to look behind me. Almost everyone in the cabin was asleep. And everyone seemed to be in an awkward position, continually shifting to try and get comfortable. I sat back down and pulled the plane blanket up over my waist.

As I tried to sleep again, I suddenly had thoughts of home. I thought of Mum and Dad, talking in the kitchen over cups of tea. I thought of Olivia, tucked up in her bed with our dog, Bob, sleeping at her feet (which he's not allowed to do). I thought of my brother, Max, snoring lightly as he slept with his lightsaber toy clutched to his chest. I thought of Zoe and Violet, back at Eden College in our half-empty dorm room. It was enough to make me feel like I was going to cry.

But then I heard the words of my intrepid Nanna Kate in my mind (*intrepid* means a brave traveller, by the way). She always says that the reason people don't go on big adventures like she does is because they are too scared to leap into the unknown, and so they miss out on the adventures life has to offer. As my eyes became heavier again, I thought how London was an unknown for me. So what adventures were awaiting me on the other side of the world?

Chapter 4

From: Ella

Sent: Monday, 8:42 PM (UTC+08:00) Singapore

To: Olivia

Subject: Hello from Singapore!

Ni hao, vanakkam and selamat hari, Olivia! That's hello in Mandarin, Tamil and Malay. Can you believe there are *three* official languages in Singapore besides English? Pretty cool, hey!

We made it to Singapore for our overnight stopover and are staying in a hotel right next to the airport, so we won't get to see any of Singapore at all.

But I'm soooo glad to be in a real bed. Sleeping on a plane is NOT fun, no, it is NOT! Remember when we went to Queensland on a plane? Well, this is nothing like that. Trying to sleep on an eight-hour plane ride is worse than trying to sleep on a half-deflated air mattress at a lumpy campsite with Max and Bob lying on top of you!

I can't wait to actually get to London and be finished with the travel!

When we arrive in London, we are going straight to the boarding school we will be staying at. It's called Crestwood Hall and is a boarding school for girls *and* boys. I don't know how I'd feel about having boys at Eden College! I'm a bit nervous about meeting the Crestwood students—I hope they are as nice as the Eden girls.

Anyway, I'd better get a good night's sleep before we are stuck on the plane for another 14 hours early tomorrow.

I'll email you again when we get to Crestwood.

Miss you!

Love, Ella

x

‘Look! It’s Buckingham Palace!’ Tilly exclaimed.

We all leapt over to the left side of the bus to get a glimpse of the famous royal palace.

‘I wonder if the Queen is home,’ Grace said eagerly.

‘Look at the guards with their fluffy hats!’ Ivy said, pointing at the guards standing stony-faced in their red coats and tall fluffy hats.

The bus drove on, curling around the River Thames, which ran right through the middle of London. Then we whizzed past a big castle with light stone walls and the flag of the United Kingdom at the top, flapping about in the breeze.

‘Is that a *real* castle?’ I asked.

‘It’s the Tower of London,’ Ivy said. ‘That’s where the Crown Jewels are kept!’

I imagined the royal jewels inside and wondered if a burglar would ever try to steal them. That would make a fabulous mystery for me to solve!

Just past the Tower of London, we could see the

famous Tower Bridge, which stretched across the Thames. I'd seen that bridge before on a postcard from my Nanna Kate, when she'd visited London a few years ago. I felt like I was living in a postcard now—everything looked so different from home. It was as if we were driving through a movie set. Except this was all real, real, REAL! I was definitely in London.

We drove out of the city centre and into a quieter part of London, with more green trees and parks. Suddenly, the bus turned off and ambled up a long curved driveway. The gravel crunched under the tyres as we slowed to a stop.

'Woah,' Grace whispered.

I'd thought Eden College was impressive. But Crestwood Hall was truly majestic. It looked like a medieval castle, with stone walls and ornate carvings all over the building (*ornate* means really detailed and fancy). The central tower had a clock built right into the stone and even a battlement at the top—that's what a book I read called the square bits that stick up from the wall. It made it look like a real-life princess castle!

I half expected there to be a drawbridge, but as we stepped off the bus, I could see there wasn't. All around the front of the school were manicured lawns with beautifully shaped hedges.

My body ached from the long flights and I had no concept of what time it was. According to my watch, it was almost bedtime back home. But the sun was blazing high in the clear blue sky. A warm summer's breeze gently blew against my arms and the scent of sweet flowers sat lightly on the wind. I wiped my tired eyes with the back of my wrist, the glare of the English summer sun making me squint.

As we lined up in front of the entrance to the castle-like school, we saw several figures come through the front archway and down the path to greet us. There was a man, wearing a crisp suit, and a woman, also in a smart skirt suit. They were followed by a boy and a girl, who looked to be Seniors.

The woman cleared her throat. 'Welcome, Eden College!'

We all waved awkwardly.

'I am Dr Smythe, the Headmistress of this school. This is Mr Pepper, the Vice Headmaster,' she said, gesturing to her left. 'And these are our two School Captains, Martin and Angela.'

'Welcome to Crestwood Hall,' Angela said, stepping forward.

'If you'd care to follow us inside, we will show you to your rooms,' Martin said, pointing his hand towards the opening of the school.

We walked through the archway and across to another large building behind the frontage of the school. As we made our way through the double doors and inside, my mouth fell open. It was regal. That means something fit for a king or queen. There were soaring columns that curved upwards towards a vaulted ceiling and huge wooden beams spanned the vast area. The adults' shoes clacked along the marble floor, only silenced when we walked over the lavish rugs or hallway runners. There was a mix of things that looked brand new and items of antiquity (which means really old). But it all somehow seemed to match.

Curious students leaned over the banisters of the upper levels, whispering and pointing at the strangers below. I suddenly felt underdressed and sloppy in my comfy travel clothes, which consisted of tracksuit pants, a t-shirt and sneakers. The girl students were wearing black and white plaid skirts with crisp, white short-sleeved blouses, as it was summer in England at this time of year. Although some of them still wore sweet little, grey buttoned cardigans with black trim. I was surprised to see some really young students, until I suddenly remembered reading that even though it was a boarding school, students could attend Crestwood Hall from the age of five. And that wasn't the only difference to Eden College. My eyes widened as I saw the boys also wandering the halls of the school, wearing long grey trousers with white shirts and red ties.

Angela and Martin pointed out a few things as they led us towards the main stairwell, but they said we would have a proper tour of the school later, when we were all settled and less tired. We stopped in front of a bunch of students at the foot of the stairs, and

Dr Smythe took out a list and began to assign us to rooms, pairing us up with a Crestwood student to show us the way. I had my fingers and toes crossed that Grace and I would be together, and breathed a heavy sigh of relief when I noticed they were keeping girls of the same year levels together. Grace and I were directed to stand with a Crestwood girl who looked about our age. She had deep, dark brown eyes and her black hair was pulled back in a long thick plait. She smiled warmly at us.

'Hello,' she said chirpily. 'I'm Sara. Welcome to Crestwood Hall!'

'I'm Ella, and this is Grace,' I said, smiling.

'Oh, I love your accents!' Sara giggled. 'You sound like something out of a movie!'

'I was thinking the same about you,' Grace said. 'You all sound so posh.'

Sara laughed. 'How old are you?' she asked.

'Twelve,' I said. 'We are in Year 7 back home, which is our first year of high school. What about you?'

'I'm 12, too. In the First Form, as we call it here.

You'll be staying in my dorm with some of the other girls in my form. Do you want to come and see?'

Grace and I nodded. I repositioned my travel backpack over my shoulder and followed Sara past the stairwell. We exited out the rear doors of the main building into a beautiful grassed quadrangle, which had covered stone paths with archways leading to other adjoining buildings. Crestwood Hall was much bigger than Eden College, I noticed. And the buildings seemed older and more imposing.

We followed Sara along one of the paths and as we passed other Crestwood students, some of them stopped and whispered and pointed at us curiously. We finally rounded a corner and entered another building.

'This is the girls' quarters,' Sara said, as she opened the big double door. 'All the girls sleep in here, and the boys sleep in matching dorms on the other side of the quadrangle.'

We followed Sara up a wide twisting flight of stairs.

'And this is our level,' she said, pointing up the corridor after we'd climbed three flights of stairs.

We walked up the carpeted hall and I noticed there were lots of old portraits hanging on the walls. Serious men and women looked down from the paintings with piercing eyes. It was almost like they didn't approve of us scraggily travellers walking their pristine halls.

Halfway down, Sara stopped and pushed open a door, beckoning for us to follow her in. I was a little taken aback when I entered. At Eden College, there were only four girls to a dorm room, so the rooms weren't that big. Our dorms just looked like large bedrooms and reminded me of home. But at Crestwood, the dormitories were huge cavernous rooms with tall ceilings and wooden beams that criss-crossed along the top. There were two rows of beds along the longer walls, and I quickly counted two, four, six, eight, ten beds in the room! Plus two additional fold-out beds down the end, which I presumed were for me and Grace.

'Oh, wow, you have lots of people to a room!' Grace said, as if reading my mind.

'Yes, about ten per dorm room,' Sara said. 'It can get a little crazy sometimes, but we're used to it. Most of us started boarding at Crestwood when we were six years old.'

I raised my eyebrows in awe. I'd thought I was brave going to Eden College at 12! I couldn't imagine being a six-year-old at boarding school. I tried to think of my little brother, Max, who was seven, going off to boarding school all alone, and I just couldn't!

The room was empty, as all the other students were in the middle of their school day. We walked down to the fold-out beds at the end of the room and put our backpacks down.

'This is where you two will sleep,' she said. 'I hope it's comfortable for you.'

I sat on the portable bed and was surprised to find it felt soft. It had a lovely quilted bedspread and a nice soft pillow.

'It feels great,' I said. But the mere touch of the pillow under my hand made me remember how tired I was, and all I wanted to do was to lie down and sleep. But Mrs Hodges had told us no napping, otherwise we would never get over our jet lag. That's what she called the tired feeling we all had from flying for so long and across different time zones.

'I'll leave you to get changed and settled,' Sara said. 'The shower block is just next door. Lunch is in the Great Hall in one hour, back near the stairwell in the main building.'

Grace and I smiled as Sara left the room.

'So, how do you like jolly old England?' Grace said, putting on her best English accent.

I laughed. 'Charming,' I said, mocking her attempt at an accent.

'How about these buildings, though?' Grace breathed. 'It's just like being in a castle! I have a feeling we are going to go on some great adventures while we are here.'

I nodded. I felt it too. It was like this country was full of mystery and intrigue. And I just knew something exciting was going to happen.

Chapter 5

We walked with tentative steps back to the Great Hall. As we peered in the door, I was stunned by the sheer number of students sitting at the long tables, which were aligned in neat rows in the vast room. Students as young as five chattered and laughed as they sat, patiently waiting to be called to line up to get their food.

'Wow, look at the lunch!' Grace whispered.

I'd heard that it was really common in England to have a hot lunch in the daytime, even in summer. Back at Eden College, we usually picked up a sandwich or wrap for lunch, or if it was a hot meal in winter it was still pasta or something we could easily take away to eat outdoors. But here I could see steaming hot slices of beef, cooked vegetables and a deep pan of gravy in the servery.

'Ella! Grace!' Sara called from the end of one of the long tables.

Mrs Hodges had urged us to get to know the Crestwood students during our stay. So Grace and I slid along the bench seat to sit next to Sara, and she looked at us like a proud parent, beaming with sparkly eyes.

'Ella, Grace, these are my friends,' she said. 'This is Archie, Sophia and Henry.'

'Hi,' Grace and I chorused nervously.

'Don't you say "G'day, mate"?' Archie asked, looking a little disappointed.

Grace laughed. 'Not everyone talks like that in Australia.'

Archie wrinkled his nose, his red glasses shifting on his face.

'What pets do you have?' Henry asked, leaning in.

'I have a dog named Bob,' I said.

'Not a kangaroo or koala?' Henry asked, also disappointed.

I giggled. 'No, but sometimes we see them in the bushland near our school.'

'Wow, cool!' Sophia said.

One of the Crestwood teachers called our table to line up and collect our hot lunch. We stood up and followed our new friends to the line, which snaked along the counter where the kitchen staff were serving. I slid my tray along the metal shelf and lifted my plate to hand to the first server. The kitchen staff scooped hot beef, peas, pumpkin and carrots onto my plate.

'Yorkie?' one of them asked, holding up a beige-coloured piece of food that I'd never seen before.

'Oh, um . . .' I looked to Sara in confusion.

'You've never had a Yorkshire pudding?!' she gasped.

'Pudding?' I said, shaking my head. 'Is it dessert?'

'No, it's like a pastry and you pour gravy all over it—it's amazing, you have to try.'

I nodded hesitantly to the kitchen staff, who put the round item onto my plate, then ladled thick brown gravy over the top.

We took our food back to our seats and sat down to eat. I nervously prodded the Yorkie with my fork.

'It's good, Ella, you need to try!' Grace said, as she stuffed a second piece of Yorkshire pudding in her mouth.

I shrugged, cut a small piece and popped it in my mouth. It was delicious! A bit like a cross between a pie crust and a pancake, and with the salty gravy it almost tasted like a meat pie. Archie, Henry, Sophia and Sara watched on for my reaction.

'It *is* good!' I laughed.

They all broke into smiles.

'You are a true English girl now,' Sara grinned.

'So, do you both have artworks in the competition?' Henry asked, as we continued to eat.

'No, just Grace,' I said proudly. 'She's amazing.'

Grace blushed.

'I'm here as a reporter for our school newspaper, so I'll still be at all the gallery events,' I added.

'Archie and I will be, too!' Sara said excitedly. 'Archie has a portrait in the competition and it's incredible. He's done a charcoal drawing of his grandfather—it's the most amazing thing I've ever seen!'

Archie shook his head, embarrassed, and pushed up his glasses nervously.

'I get to come because I am the official Year 7 buddy and tour guide,' Sara added. 'It's my job to make sure you and Grace don't get lost in London!'

A warm feeling flooded into my chest. I was so excited to explore the city, and I felt safer knowing we had a local to show us around.

'Tomorrow will be our first day at the gallery,' Sara continued. 'We get to help set up the exhibition, which officially opens to the public the day after. It will be on display for a week, and then the judges will announce the winner of the competition at a special awards ceremony. After that, all your Eden College art will be packed up and shipped back to Australia, where you will have your own exhibition in your state gallery.'

'It all sounds so official!' Grace laughed nervously. 'Like a real art show.'

'It *is* a real art show,' Henry said. 'Your work will

be hanging in one of our most famous art galleries—alongside some of the most valuable pieces of art in the world.'

Archie grimaced and lifted his fork, full of peas, to his mouth, just as someone walking behind him bumped his head with their arm. His peas went scattering across the table.

'Hey!' Archie said, whirling around.

'Oh, I'm sorry, I must have slipped,' a tall boy said with a smirk on his face. Two other boys standing behind him laughed mockingly.

'Leave him alone, Kai,' Sara said, sitting up straight.

'Who asked you?' Kai sneered. He turned to face Archie again. 'See you at the gallery.' Kai stalked away as Archie gathered his spilt peas from the table. He focused his eyes on his plate, his cheeks burning red.

'Who was that?' Grace asked.

'That's Kai. He's in Second Form, your Year 8, and he thinks he owns this school. He's always giving the younger students a hard time,' Sophia said, frowning.

'Especially me,' Archie muttered.

'And, annoyingly, he has a portrait in the art competition, so we'll have to put up with him all week,' Sara said.

'Yeah, a portrait of himself!' Henry added, laughing. 'He actually painted a portrait of himself in his rugby gear, standing on the pitch as if he's some kind of god.'

I rolled my eyes. 'He sounds horrible,' I said, looking over to where Kai was standing in the food line, waiting to get his lunch. He stood tall and flicked his brown fringe back with a whip of his head. Then he said something to his friends and laughed loudly at his own joke. I wrinkled my nose and made a mental note to keep as far away from that boy as I could.

I looked back at Archie, who still had his head down, staring into his lunch.

'You know what my Nanna Kate says?' I said to him. Archie looked up. 'She says people are often meanest when they are threatened by you. Your artwork must be pretty great for an older boy to want to make you feel bad.'

'Do you think?' Archie said, unsure.

'Yep. Why else would he want to get you down? He's obviously trying to get in your head before the competition,' I said matter-of-factly.

Archie paused. 'You know, he's only been targeting me since they made the announcement about my work representing the Crestwood First Form in the art show.'

'See?' Grace said, joining in. 'You've clearly got this, Archie!'

Archie smiled at me, and my cheeks reddened.

Then a bell pierced the air and everyone began shuffling around, clearing their plates and taking them up to the servery.

'That's the warning bell,' Sara said. 'It means we have to be in class in five minutes.'

'We have our own Eden College meeting now, too,' Grace said, standing up and promptly dropping her knife, which clattered to the floor. 'Oops!'

'See you later, then,' Sophia said.

'Great to meet you!' Henry said.

Archie waved, and they turned and walked away.

Chapter 6

'Stay together!' Mrs Hodges called.

We continued to follow her in a long line—a mix of Eden College and Crestwood Hall students, walking along the streets of London. I breathed in deeply. It smelt different to the city back home—damp, even though the sun was shining. The noise of cars and buses filled the air, and snippets of conversation in English accents floated past me. I watched a red double-decker bus amble up the street, followed by the cutest, little black taxicab, which looked like something a quaint old-fashioned butler would drive around in. Up ahead, a towering billboard advertised the latest musical playing in the West End.

We passed tourist shops with t-shirts hanging in the window saying 'I ♥ London'. Key rings with Big Ben, that famous clock, dangled from racks, along with little bears in beefeater uniforms. *Beefeaters* is the nickname for the ceremonial guards at the Tower of London, and they have the sweetest frilly collars and rosettes on their hats and shoes.

'Is that the Underground?' I asked Sara, pointing to a set of stairs in the ground next to a sign with a red circle on it. The Underground was the system of train lines which commuted people around the city, and I recognised the trademark red circle logo.

'Sure is,' Sara said. 'We call it the Tube for short.'

The English summer sun felt warm through my blazer, but there was a nice cool breeze blowing. Whenever we were going to the gallery or any kind of formal event during our stay in London, we had been instructed to wear our Eden College summer uniform, including our blue blazers, so we could 'represent the school with pride', as Ms Montgomery had said. Lucky it was nowhere near as hot as summer back home, or we'd be roasting!

As we approached the gallery, Grace turned to me with wide eyes. I think she couldn't quite believe that her artwork was going to be displayed in such a fancy building. The gallery had cascading stone steps, which led up to the giant sandstone building. The entrance was flanked by tall columns and big metal doors. We all walked up together and entered into the cool of the foyer, with its marble floor. In the centre of the foyer was a large stone statue of a lion, sitting up on its haunches, glaring down at us.

A gallery attendant in a uniform bustled over to us.

'You must be some of our guests for the interschool art competition exhibition!' she gushed excitedly.

'Yes, we are from Crestwood Hall and Eden College,' Mrs Hodges said.

'Well, welcome,' the woman smiled. 'My name is Margaret and I've been working in this gallery for over 40 years.' Margaret had a warm voice and happy eyes, like my Nanna Kate, and was probably a similar age. She caught my eye and winked at me.

'We've just finished setting up the exhibit with the artworks from all the participating schools,' Margaret said, bobbing up and down on her heels. 'If you'd like to follow me, I'll take you through for a look.'

Margaret and the teachers handed out lanyards to each of us, which had a barcode on them so that we could go past gallery security without buying a ticket. We had free access to the art gallery for the entire week. We walked in single file through the scanners, the security guard nodding at us as the scanner made a light clicking noise each time someone passed through.

Then we followed Margaret into a big open room. On the far wall, there was a large banner saying, 'International Student Portrait Prize' and the walls were covered in the art of students from near and far. I reached into my tote bag and pulled out my notebook and pen. If I was going to be reporting on the artworks for Eden Press, I'd better start gathering details.

'Grace, look!' I heard Sara call from the other side of

the room. We turned and saw Grace's artwork hanging proudly on the wall. It had been set in an ornate gold frame and there was a small light shining down on it. The colours seemed to emanate off the walls and sparkle (*emanate* is a fancy word for flowing out of). Even Grace looked a little shocked at her own work.

'That's amazing, Grace!' Archie said, tilting his head to the side.

'Where's yours?' Grace asked.

Archie looked around the room, searching for his work. 'There it is!'

We all walked over to where Archie's charcoal drawing was hanging in the corner of the room. Despite being all black, the drawing almost looked alive. Archie had sketched his grandfather in tremendous detail—you could see every wrinkle on his face. His eyes were warm and communicated his long life story.

'That's incredible,' I breathed.

'Thanks, Ella,' Archie said proudly.

'Oh, good, I'm next to a rubbish artwork. That'll help my chances of winning,' a snide voice said behind us.

Kai looked at Archie's work as if it had a bad smell coming out of it.

'Who made you the King of England?' Grace said forcefully.

Archie shot a look at Grace, silently pleading with her not to goad Kai.

'And where's *your* artwork, little girl?' Kai sneered.

Grace coolly raised an eyebrow and pointed proudly at her work. Kai looked at it and his eyes widened as he took it in. Grace smiled smugly, sensing that Kai was secretly impressed.

But Kai quickly shook his head and turned to his own painting, hanging next to Archie's, and breathed in deeply, saying, '*This* is real art.'

We all looked at Kai's painting. It *was* pretty good, I had to admit. But as Henry had said the day before, Kai had painted a portrait of himself on the rugby pitch. The angle of the painting was from the ground, meaning that we were looking up to Kai, his body towering over the viewer in a powerful pose. He had even painted a light shining behind him, which seemed to bounce off his shoulders. He really did look like some kind of demi-god. I rolled my eyes.

'Come on, guys. Let's look at the other pieces,' Sara said, pulling lightly at Archie's sleeve. Kai scoffed as we all sidled away.

As we walked around the room, I jotted down notes on the art hanging in the exhibition. There was such a range of styles and techniques. I couldn't understand how the judges were going to assess them all when they were all so different. I stopped in front of one and stared, wondering what the story behind it was. But my focus broke when I heard a shuffle next to me. I looked up and saw the gallery assistant, Margaret, frowning slightly at me. She quickly smiled when we locked eyes.

'And who is this little reporter?' she asked, nodding down at my notebook.

'I'm Ella,' I said. 'I'm from Eden College and I'm reporting on the competition for our school newspaper.'

Margaret smiled and nodded. 'Ah, a journalist. How exciting! You look like someone who is always searching for a story.'

I blushed. 'I do love getting to the bottom of things!'

Margaret nodded silently. 'I always loved writing when I was a child, too. Nobody could ever sneak anything past me without me noticing!'

'That's what my Nanna Kate says about me, too,' I laughed.

'I can help you if you like,' Margaret said. 'I know everything about this gallery and all the exhibitions in it. I've worked here for more than half my life.'

'That would be incredible,' I said eagerly. Margaret was bound to have some interesting stories as well as inside knowledge of everything in the gallery.

'My pleasure,' Margaret said, her grey curls bouncing around her beaming face. 'Let's stick together a bit then. I can point out things of interest for you and give you some extra content for your report. When you come into the gallery each day, come and find me. I can even give you a tour of some other areas that aren't accessible to the public.'

'Wow, thanks!' I said, as Archie, Sara and Grace came over to join us.

'And these must be your friends?' Margaret asked.

'Yes, this is Grace, Archie and Sara. Grace's artwork is that one over there,' I said, pointing to the opposite wall, 'and Archie's is the amazing charcoal drawing over there in the corner.'

'Ah, such talent!' Margaret gushed. 'Are you all from the Australian school?'

'No, just me and Grace. Sara and Archie go to Crestwood Hall here in London,' I said.

Margaret nodded. 'Well, it's a pleasure to meet you. I look forward to showing you around the gallery more.'

Margaret smiled and waved, before walking over to talk to another group of students.

'She's so nice,' Sara said.

'Yes, and she said she can tell us everything about what goes on in the gallery. She can even give us access to restricted areas! It's just what I need to write an amazing story for Eden Press,' I said, feeling the excitement bubble up inside me.

Yes, Margaret could be exactly what I needed to get that extra special story I was looking for.

Chapter 7

From: Ella

Sent: Thursday, 8:26 AM (UTC+01:00) London

To: Olivia

Subject: Hello from London!

Hi Olivia,

I'm sure Mum told you I've arrived in London. This place is incredible! It's just like all the English movies we've ever watched. Everyone sounds so posh, but they think we are the ones with the funny accents!

We spent yesterday morning at the art gallery where the

exhibit is being held, and I met a really nice lady named Margaret, who works there. She was telling me all the inside goss about the gallery. Did you know they have a security guard there 24 hours a day?! She said it's to stop people from trying to steal the priceless artworks. She's also going to show me a painting that's worth millions of dollars!

After the gallery, we got to go on a tour of Buckingham Palace. That's where the Queen sometimes lives! We saw some of the State Rooms, which are sooo sumptuous (that's a word for super fancy, in case you didn't know), and we even saw the Throne Room, with the Queen's very own throne! There were so many fancy pieces of art all over the palace, too.

Today we have a free day, and Sara and Archie, our new English friends, are going to take us into the city centre to look around and to pick up some supplies. We are making a banner with the rest of the Crestwood Hall art students for the exhibit award ceremony next week, but we need more pink paint. One of the Senior girls is going to take us on the Tube!

I have to go so I can email Zoe and Violet before we leave and let them know what we've been up to as well.

Love, Ella

xx

The air whipped through my hair as the bus gained speed.

'This is so fun!' I laughed.

Archie, Grace, Sara and I were being accompanied by a Senior Crestwood Hall girl named Lottie. She was happy to be our tour guide, because it meant she got to skip classes for the day. Sara was also allowed to miss classes as our buddy, and Archie too, since he was part of the art competition. I was so excited to be out in London with my friends.

We'd decided to travel around on a special tour bus. It was one of those red double-decker buses I'd seen, but the top level had no roof. It meant we could see all the sights of London as the bus driver pointed things out over a loudspeaker. We were also able to hop on and off the bus as much as we liked, stopping at different landmarks along the way, then jumping onto the next open-air tour bus that came along.

For Archie and Sara, it was completely normal to be travelling around the big bustling city of London, and they seemed to know all the streets and shops like it was home. But I felt like a real-life traveller and a proper grown-up, exploring the city without a teacher or parent. It even felt like we were out alone, because Lottie barely spoke to us, and spent the whole time looking down at her phone.

We hopped off the tour bus at Big Ben, which is the famous clock tower. I took a selfie of me, Sara, Grace and Archie in front of it.

'Grace, can you take one of just me for my Nanna Kate?' I asked.

Grace took my phone and I posed with the towering clock in the background and smiled.

'There you go!' she said, handing me back my phone. 'Ooh, what's that big Ferris wheel?' Grace pointed to a huge wheel with enclosed compartments on the other side of the river.

'That's the London Eye,' Archie said. 'It gives the best views of London. Do you want to go for a ride?'

Grace's face turned slightly green. 'I'm not great with heights,' she murmured.

I always found it a bit odd that Grace was afraid of heights. She was usually such a daredevil. But as Nanna Kate says, everyone has their insecurities in life, even the most confident people.

'The compartments are completely closed,' Sara said. 'So you won't be out in the air. It's more like being inside a building that happens to move.'

Grace thought for a moment, then nodded. 'OK, I'll give it a try,' she smiled.

We ran across the Westminster Bridge to the bottom of the London Eye and bought a ticket. Thankfully, it wasn't so busy being a weekday. As we moved to the front of the line, a large pod circled down and the door swung open. It was fairly spacious and fit about 20 people inside. Most of the capsule was made of glass, which meant we could look out in any direction.

Lottie had decided not to join us on the ride, so it was just Sara, Grace, Archie and I in the pod. Slowly, the door closed and we began to move. I peered out of the windows excitedly. I could see the River Thames flowing beneath us, and Big Ben standing opposite us. Adjoining the towering clock was a fancy yellow building that looked like a palace.

'What's that?' I asked, pointing to it.

'That's the Palace of Westminster,' Archie said, adjusting his glasses on his nose. 'But most people call it the Houses of Parliament, because that's where our parliament meets.'

The capsule rose higher and higher, the murky River Thames becoming smaller and smaller below and London spreading out around us. I turned to Grace, who looked a little pale.

'Are you OK?' I asked. It was a long way down.

'I'm OK,' she said. 'But I think I'll stand in the middle of the capsule instead of right up at the window's edge!'

The blue sky stretched out ahead of us, and I felt like I was flying. I pulled out my phone and took some photos of the view. Then I gathered Sara and Archie for a photo.

'Come over too, Grace,' I said.

'OK, but I'm not looking down!' she said shakily.

I pulled my friends into a huddle and we all smiled as I snapped a selfie with the view of London in the background.

The wheel slowly ambled around as we descended back to the ground. I could see Lottie sitting on a bench waiting for us, but she didn't see us wave because her eyes were glued to her phone. When the capsule slowed to a stop, the doors swung open and Grace took a big relieved breath.

'It's so good to be back on the ground!' she breathed.

'Good on you for conquering your fear,' I laughed, giving her a little side hug. 'I think we need to remember this moment.' Lottie finally looked up from her phone, and I gestured for her to come over. 'Lottie, can you take a pic?'

Lottie rolled her eyes and took my phone. She snapped the photo apathetically (which means she didn't really care) and handed the phone back to me.

'Thanks!' I said. 'What now?'

'I don't know about you, but I'm starving,' Archie moaned.

'There's an art shop not far from here,' Sara said. 'Let's go pick up the paint supplies for our banner, then jump back on the open-top bus to Trafalgar Square, where we can eat lunch.'

Grace and I nodded excitedly. I'd seen Trafalgar Square in photos of London before.

'Is that OK, Lottie?' Sara asked. Lottie just shrugged nonchalantly (which, again, means she didn't really care) and went back to her phone.

We bought the paint and jumped back on the bus. As we crossed over the river again, we decided to get out at the Strand and walk the rest of the way to Trafalgar Square through the West End.

'Wow!' I breathed as we passed theatre after theatre. This was where all the famous London musicals were performed. There were bright shining signs for *Cats, Phantom of the Opera, Matilda the Musical* and *West Side Story*. One of the signs had a dark leafy border all around it and I gasped in amazement when I realised what musical it was for.

'It's *Enchantment the Musical*!' I shrieked.

'Ella was one of the dryads when our school performed this musical last term,' Grace explained to the others.

'We have to beg Mrs Hodges to let us come and see it before we go!' I said.

We kept walking along the Strand until we reached Trafalgar Square. It was a large open area, with a big flowing fountain in the centre. We stood at the base of a huge lion statue, which looked just like Aslan from the *Narnia* books I used to read.

'Dare me to climb it?' Grace laughed mischievously.

Before I could say anything, Grace had hoisted herself up onto the back of the lion.

'Come on!' she yelled.

Archie gave me a boost and Grace held out her hand

to help me up behind her. I dangled my legs on either side of the huge lion's body.

Sara and Archie pulled themselves up behind me too, so we were all sitting in a conga line.

'Take a photo, Lottie!' Sara yelled, tossing Lottie her phone.

Lottie rolled her eyes.

'Say "London",' she said flatly.

'LONDON!' we all cheered as she snapped the shot.

We found somewhere to get lunch and decided to order hot chips to takeaway so we could eat them at the fountain.

'Vinegar?' the man at the counter asked.

I looked at Sara, shocked. *'Vinegar?!'* I echoed, scrunching up my nose.

'Yes, please! It's the best!' Sara said, as the man at the counter sprinkled the clear liquid all over her chips. 'Come on, you have to try it—it's an English delicacy.'

Vinegar was so strong—I couldn't think how it would be nice on my chips. But I reluctantly agreed.

We carried our containers over to the big fountain

and perched ourselves on the rim. I pulled out one of my chips, covered in salt and sodden with vinegar, and gingerly took a bite.

'Not bad,' I said, shrugging. 'Gives it a nice tang.'

After we finished our lunch, Sara gathered up the rubbish and took it to the bin. Then we sat, basking in the summer sun. I dipped my fingers into the fountain, which flowed with cool clear water.

'It's so hot,' Sara sighed. 'I wish we were allowed to swim in the fountain.'

'This is not even hot,' Grace said, laughing slightly. 'This is spring weather in Australia. Sometimes we have days that are over 40 degrees!'

Archie's eyes widened. 'Surely you'd melt?!'

I laughed. 'It's not nice, but thankfully Eden College is pretty well air conditioned. And we have the pool, too.'

'What do you want to do this arvo?' Grace asked.

'Arvo?' Sara laughed.

'It means afternoon,' I clarified. 'It's very Australian to shorten every word you can.'

‘Arvo, servo, sanga, cuppa, bickie, footy . . .’ Every time Grace said another word, Sara and Archie laughed harder and harder.

‘Speak English!’ Archie hooted.

When our sides started to ache, we calmed down a little.

‘We need to do the banner this afternoon, remember?’ Sara said, gesturing towards the art supplies in the bag by our feet.

‘Oh, yeah! Let me see the paint,’ Grace said, clapping excitedly.

Sara passed her the bag and she pulled out the big jug of paint labelled ‘Ethereal Rose’. *Ethereal* means heavenly.

‘I *LOVE* paint,’ Grace said, gently unscrewing the lid.

‘Don’t spill it on yourself,’ Archie warned.

‘It’s such a nice colour. And now we don’t have to mix our own. There’s heaps here, which should cover most of the background of the banner,’ Grace said. She balanced the jug on the side of the fountain and dipped her pinky finger in the paint. Then she reached out and dotted it on my nose.

'Hey!' I protested.

I reached out to grab the jug, but Grace stood up on the edge of the fountain and picked it up, holding it above her head.

'Give it here—you can't be trusted!' I teased.

'Careful, Grace,' Archie warned, as Grace teetered back on the fountain's edge.

But it was too late.

Grace swayed on her feet as her back arched and her free arm swung around in circles, trying to regain her balance.

'Grace!' I shrieked, right as she toppled backwards into the fountain.

SPLASH!

Not only did she fall into the fountain, but she tipped two litres of paint in with her.

'The paint!' Sara yelled, as Grace sat up in the fountain, gasping, her clothes dripping off her.

She reached for the jug, but it was much too late.

Huge glugs of paint had already poured out of the jug, turning the clear fountain water pink.

Crowds of people came over to look, the kids screaming with delight as the pink water frothed out the top of the fountain.

'Oh, Grace,' I said, shaking my head.

Then, two English policemen stepped out of the crowd.

'Uh-oh,' Sara mumbled.

Grace looked at them apologetically. 'Oops?' she offered.

Chapter 8

Thankfully, we didn't get into *too* much trouble for the pink fountain incident. The police constables, as they are called in England, understood it was an accident. But the next day, there was an article about it in all the newspapers and online, with photos of the pink Trafalgar fountain. Everyone at Crestwood Hall was talking about it, and we were so embarrassed.

We didn't have any organised activities until the afternoon, when Mrs Hodges was going to take the Eden girls to another famous art gallery called the Tate. So we decided to get away from school and go visit our own gallery exhibit—it was too embarrassing with everyone calling us 'Pinky' all morning.

We walked through the bustling tunnels of the underground train station, which were heaving with commuters on their way to work. Buskers strummed guitars and sang, and the smell of hot food, sweat and a little bit of smoke filled the air. I wrinkled my nose—the smells of the city. We rode the steep escalator up to the top and exited into the warm summer sun. I breathed in deeply, happy to be out of the underground maze, which always made me feel a little like a rat in a sewer.

Archie, Sara, Grace, Lottie and I walked along the street, often having to fall into single file to navigate our way through the crowds. As we approached the gallery, I fished in my tote bag to find my entry tag lanyard, and looped it around my neck.

We walked through the security checkpoint and headed straight over to the student exhibition area, where Margaret was bustling around. When she saw us, her face lit up into a smile.

'Good morning, children!' she sang happily.

'Good morning, Margaret,' we chorused.

'What happened?' Sara asked, frowning as she looked around. The exhibit looked different to when we'd last seen it.

'After you all came in on Wednesday, we rearranged the artworks for the competition,' Margaret said. 'They are now more logically grouped for the judges and it's a better flow through the exhibit for viewers, too.'

We all nodded.

'But I have some exciting news,' Margaret beamed. 'The new Renaissance art exhibition has arrived! It has some priceless works in it. It's not yet open to the public, but would you like a sneak peek?'

We exchanged glances and broke into smiles. 'Yes, please!' we chorused.

Lottie murmured a quiet protest.

'You don't have to come if you don't want to,' Margaret whispered to Lottie, sensing her lack of interest in hanging out with us Junior students. 'I'll take care of them. Go grab a cup of tea in the café.'

Lottie's eyes lit up and she thanked Margaret.

She'd probably spend the next hour on her phone.

We walked across the marble floors to a door marked 'Staff Only'. Margaret had to swipe her security tag to get us access, and we followed her up two flights of stairs and out into another hallway.

'The works are hanging in the main gallery, but we are keeping it roped off until the grand opening,' she explained.

We approached a doorway, where two security guards stood.

'Hi, Margaret,' one of them said cheerily.

'Hi, Geoff,' she replied, smiling widely. 'I hope you don't mind, but I wanted to give my special little friends here a sneak peek at the Renaissance exhibit.'

Geoff smiled a crooked grin. 'Well, that's not completely in line with protocol, but as long as I can scan your passes, we'll have a record of who has been in here. Besides, it's quite the show.' He winked at us. 'But remember, kids, *do not* touch anything!'

We all nodded eagerly, silently promising to be on our best behaviour.

'Geoff has twin daughters your age,' Margaret whispered. 'I just knew he'd have a soft spot for you all.'

Geoff scanned Margaret's pass and then each of our lanyard access tags, before we walked into the exhibition room. The walls were covered in huge paintings, which all seemed to be in a similar realistic style.

'What are Renaissance paintings?' I asked Margaret, pulling out my notebook and pen to take notes.

'The Renaissance was an era in European history,' Margaret explained, 'in the 1400s and 1500s. It was an important time for art and philosophy, and some of the most famous painters were at work during this time. You've all heard of the *Mona Lisa* by Leonardo Da Vinci?'

We nodded.

'That's a good example of a Renaissance art piece.'

'Is the *Mona Lisa* here?' Sara asked excitedly.

Margaret chuckled. 'Oh no, of course not! The *Mona Lisa* is kept in the Louvre in Paris. But we do have some other incredibly valuable paintings in this exhibit.'

Margaret beckoned us to follow her over to one particular painting. It featured sweet little cherubim (which is a fancy word for little angels) flying around a woman, who was looking out at us serenely. The painting was smaller than the others and, in some ways, less impressive. It didn't have a big gaudy frame, and it's size made me think that it probably wasn't worth as much as the others.

'This work is called *The Holy Cherubim*,' Margaret said, 'and it is worth eight million pounds —that's about 16 million dollars. It's the most valuable painting here.'

Grace spluttered as though choking. *'Sixteen million?!'*

Margaret chuckled and nodded.

I hurriedly wrote down some notes about the painting in my notebook. I'd never seen such an expensive piece of art in real life. To think that this one little painting could buy a whole block of houses or an infinity-supply of ice cream! I looked back up at the painted woman. Her milky eyes were calm and reassuring and made me feel peaceful.

It reminded me of that time Nanna Kate and I visited

an antique show. We saw all types of expensive-looking things—beautiful glittery necklaces and ornate pieces of furniture. But when the evaluator came (that's the person who tells you how much everything is worth), he focused his attention on a tiny wooden clown. The paint had scuffed off his little face and his legs hung haphazardly as he slumped against a box. Turned out that wooden clown was worth over ten thousand dollars—more than anything else in the show. I remember looking at his faded cheeky eyes and sly grin. It was like he knew he was hiding a valuable secret.

'Sixteen million . . .' Sara repeated, jolting me back to the present. 'Is that why we are being watched so closely?' With a wry smile, she nodded her head in the direction of the two security guards, who had not taken their eyes off us since we'd entered the room.

'Indeed,' Margaret said.

'What other kinds of security do you have for these types of priceless artworks?' I asked, my pen poised over my notebook.

Margaret hesitated for half a second. 'Well, they

are all microchipped for a start,' she said slowly. 'They can't leave this building without setting off a whole heap of alarms and security features. If someone tried to take these out of the gallery, doors would shut and lock, alarms would blare and the police would be alerted directly. I don't think a thief would get very far.'

I scribbled notes eagerly. This would make for a great article for Eden Press—an inside scoop on how a famous art gallery kept all their priceless art safe.

We wandered around, looking at the other works in the exhibition, until Geoff nervously told us that we'd better make our way back downstairs. Margaret thanked him and we all scanned our passes again as we walked out of the room.

'That was amazing,' Archie said softly. 'It's so weird to think that those painting were done by real people, hundreds of years ago!'

'And how cool is it to think that your and Grace's work is hanging in the same gallery as those famous Renaissance artists!' I gushed. 'Thank you for showing us, Margaret.'

We exited the stairwell and found ourselves back on the ground floor of the gallery.

'Let's go back to our exhibit and check out the new layout,' Grace said excitedly.

We followed Margaret across the marble floors, our school shoes *click-clacking*, and collected Lottie from the café, just as she was finishing her last sips of tea. Then we headed back over to our exhibition room. As we entered, I decided I wanted to make a note of each artwork in the competition, so I would be ready for when they announced the winner.

I started on the closest wall, noting down each artwork's title, artist and what the little blurb said about the piece. I also tried to note down the style of the artwork and took a photo of each on my phone.

Sara, Archie, Grace and Lottie wandered around as well, pausing at different artworks and taking in their meaning. Margaret stood in the doorway, smiling approvingly.

As I made my way through the last few pieces, Grace wandered up to me with a furrowed brow.

'Ella,' she said slowly and quietly.

I was immediately concerned. Grace so rarely looked that worried.

'Are you OK?' I asked quickly. 'Do you feel sick?'

'No, but my artwork. It's . . . it's not here.'

I looked wildly around the room. Then I looked over the list I'd just made of all the artworks. She was right—it wasn't there. But how could that be?

'What's wrong?' Sara said, coming over with Archie.

'Grace's artwork is missing,' I said flatly, still scanning my eyes around the room.

Archie's eyes widened.

'Margaret,' Sara called, beckoning the gallery attendant over to us. 'Grace's artwork isn't here!'

Margaret looked shocked. 'Well, that's not possible. We reordered them Wednesday afternoon before the exhibit officially opened to the public Thursday morning. None were taken away in the reshuffle, and none could have gone missing after the exhibit opened or there would be a blank space on the wall.'

Margaret hurriedly shuffled around the gallery walls, checking each work.

'It was the surrealist one, wasn't it? The brightly coloured one of the young boy?' Margaret said.

Grace nodded.

'This can't be,' she mumbled, as she checked each work again.

But as we lapped around the room one final time, it became clear to us all.

Grace's artwork was nowhere to be found.

Chapter 9

Grace stared vacantly into thin air. Her eyes were red and raw from crying. I'd never seen her like this. My hand lay gently on her knee, while she took a long sip of tea.

We'd searched everywhere in the gallery, with Margaret's help. She took us to all the exhibition rooms, the storerooms and even the main office. But Grace's painting wasn't in any of them.

Margaret had alerted the Head of Exhibitions at the gallery and they had called the Headmistress of Crestwood Hall to tell her and Mrs Hodges. The gallery staff had promised to search high and low to get to the bottom of the mystery. But after our own search of the gallery, my hopes were not high. We'd come back to Crestwood Hall to wait, and Mrs Hodges had excused us from the afternoon's organised excursion since Grace was so distraught (which means upset).

'I mean, what's the point of me even staying in London if I don't have a piece in the art show?' Grace sniffed.

'The competition isn't for several days yet,' Archie said soothingly. 'There's still time to find it.'

'Yeah,' Sara added. 'It's not like it grew legs and walked out of the building.'

'And the gallery staff said they'd keep looking,' I agreed.

'Yeah, right,' Grace sniffed. 'As if they care about a kid's stupid painting. They are too busy looking after million-dollar artworks.'

'Well, then maybe we need to investigate ourselves,' I said slowly.

'Really?' Grace asked, brightening slightly.

‘Yes, it’ll be just like a *Millie Mysteries*!’ Sara said, getting excited.

‘Oh, you read *Millie Mysteries*, too?’ I gushed. *Millie Mysteries* were my absolute favourite books.

‘Of course we do!’ Archie said. ‘They’re so good!’

‘Then let’s get started!’ I said firmly.

I dashed upstairs from the common area and into our dorm room. Finding my bag, I pulled out my laptop, then bounded back down the winding staircase. I burst back into the lounge where my friends were sitting waiting.

‘Right,’ I said, flipping open my computer. ‘Let’s start with the basics.’ I typed the heading in a new document: ‘The Case of the Missing Artwork’. ‘When did we last see Grace’s artwork and what events took place prior to it disappearing?’

‘The last time we know for sure Grace’s artwork was there was when we all saw it on Wednesday morning, right? Then Margaret said the gallery staff took all the artworks down on Wednesday afternoon to re-order them on the walls before the exhibit opened for the public,’ Archie said logically.

I nodded and typed it down.

'And Grace's painting can't have been there when the exhibit opened to the public, otherwise there would have been a blank space on the wall from where it was taken. So, something happened to it either after we left the gallery on Wednesday or overnight before the gallery opened Thursday morning,' Sara said.

'We need a list of who visited the gallery after we left,' I said, tapping my chin in thought.

'How do we get that?' Grace asked. 'Margaret wouldn't know anybody's names, even if she saw them in there, and our access passes aren't linked to our names.'

'Let's check the logbook!' Archie said, standing up excitedly. 'We have to sign out every time we leave the Crestwood campus, including the time and where we are going. We can see which students were at the gallery after us!'

'It won't tell us if anyone from the public was there, but it will show which *students* were there!' Sara agreed. 'Even if they aren't suspects, they may have seen something. We can interview them like real detectives!'

We all stood up with renewed energy and ran out of the common room. We walked up the hallway to the small office at the front of the main building, where a large book sat on a table. Archie opened it and scanned through the list. It had the dates, times and names of who was going out and where they were going. It even listed which Senior student was accompanying them, and then what time they got back.

'Let's see—so Sara and I signed back in at 2:30 PM on Wednesday, cause us Crestwood students didn't go on the Buckingham Palace tour with you, which means we probably all left the gallery at about 2:00 PM. The painting was still there at that time. Margaret said they rearranged the art later that afternoon. And the gallery closes at 5:00 PM. So, I think we need to check who was there between 2:00 PM and 5:00 PM,' Archie said, turning the pages back to Wednesday.

Sara leaned over his shoulder. 'Some of the girls from the Fourth Form were there at that time. Ella, make a note to interview the Fourth Form art girls.'

I opened my laptop on the table and started to type up more notes.

'Oh, and hang on,' Archie said, scrunching up his nose. 'That's interesting.'

'What? What is it?' Grace asked breathlessly.

'Look who was out of the school right before closing time at the gallery,' he said, pointing to one of the entries.

The name leapt off the page.

Kai.

'He could have been anywhere, though—it doesn't say he was at the gallery,' Sara said. The 'destination' column in the ledger was blank.

'Yes, but he only got back to school at 5:30 PM. That means if he *was* at the gallery, he was there right up until it closed,' Archie whispered.

'Why would he go back after he'd been there all morning? And why would he be there so late?' I asked.

'Here's another interesting thing,' Archie said, running his finger along the line entry. 'He hasn't listed a Senior student as accompanying him.'

'Is that allowed?' Grace asked.

Archie shook his head. 'He's only in Second Form. You need to be in Fourth Form to go out without a Senior. And look at the entries around his name—they are all at different times and none of those people are his friends. I think he went out alone, and he didn't want anyone to know where he went.'

We all looked at each other with wide eyes.

'Kai did seem nervous about your artwork,' I said slowly to Grace. 'You don't think he stole it to remove you from the competition, do you?'

Grace shrugged. We couldn't rule it out. Kai seemed like a pretty nasty person.

'What do we do now?' I asked, shutting the lid of my laptop.

'We need to talk to Kai,' Sara said firmly.

'No way,' Archie said, shaking his head. 'He's not going to just admit it to us.'

'We'll ask general questions,' Sara said. 'We won't accuse him.'

Archie didn't look convinced. 'Well,' he said, looking at his watch. 'There's only one place he would be at this time of the afternoon, and that's rugby training.'

'Let's go then!' Grace said.

Archie frowned nervously.

We headed out of the building and through a covered walkway. Sara led the way, as we followed a path that snaked its way down a hill to a lush green oval. Sure enough, it was full of boys and girls doing rugby training. And in the middle of the field was the tall commanding presence of Kai. He booted the ball into a sky-scraping bomb, then ran and caught it again in his arms, hugging it to his chest. He smiled victoriously, clearly approving of his own skills. We walked up the sideline until we were in line with him.

'Kai!' Sara yelled. 'We need to talk to you!'

Kai looked over at us and pulled a face, as if we'd asked him to pick up dog poo.

'Can't you see I'm busy training,' he snapped, kicking the ball high into the air and catching it once more.

'Well, if you don't want us to draw attention to the fact that you went out alone Wednesday afternoon, I suggest you come over,' Sara said loudly.

Archie hit his head with his palm. 'Subtle!' he muttered.

Kai looked alarmed and waved his hands in a downward motion, telling us to be quiet. He jogged over.

'Keep it down,' he hissed. 'What do you want?'

Sara smirked. She knew she had him. 'Where were you Wednesday afternoon?'

'None of your business,' he said.

'Out without a chaperone *and* refusing to say where. You'd better hope the teachers don't look too closely at the logbook,' I said.

'Were you at the gallery?' Grace asked.

'Maybe,' Kai said, his cheeks reddening.

'Where else would you have been?' Sara said.

Kai seemed to think for a moment. 'OK, yes, I was at the gallery then. I just wanted to check on my work.'

I narrowed my eyes. 'Did you see anything . . . suspicious?'

'No. I checked my work, then I left. End of story,' he said, turning back towards the pitch.

'You seemed pretty interested in Grace's artwork the other day,' Sara said. 'Almost like you were worried about competing against it.'

'Look,' Kai yelled angrily, 'I have no idea where Grace's artwork went. I had nothing to do with it. Now you losers better leave me alone if you know what's good for you.'

Kai turned and booted the ball across the oval, then chased after it like a dog chasing a stick.

'Interesting,' Archie murmured.

'What?' Grace asked. 'He didn't tell us anything.'

'Have any of you told any other students about the missing artwork?' Archie asked, his eyebrows raised.

We all looked at each other with wide eyes and shook our heads.

'Then how did he even know it was missing?' I breathed.

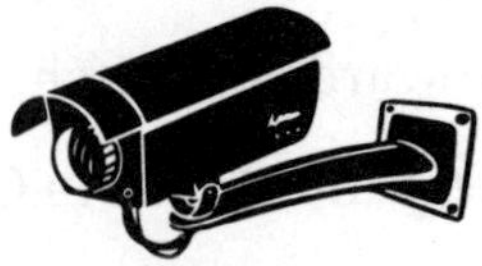

Chapter 10

The next day, we headed back to the gallery. We wanted to do some more investigating, and Mrs Hodges was going in to check on the rest of the exhibit, so we didn't need to be accompanied by Lottie. Mrs Hodges was happy for us to look around the gallery ourselves, as long as we didn't leave the building and stuck together.

We eagerly ran up to Margaret, who was on the information desk that day.

'Any news?' Grace asked hopefully.

Margaret shook her head sadly. 'Nothing yet, I'm afraid. But we're still looking!'

‘Isn’t there some kind of security footage or something we can review?’ Archie asked.

Margaret told us to go and see Geoff, the security guard, and ask him if he had found anything on the gallery surveillance.

Geoff was sitting at the entrance scanner and waved to us happily.

‘Hi, kids,’ he said.

‘Any news on Grace’s missing art?’ Sara asked.

Geoff motioned for us to come behind his desk, which had several small TV monitors on it.

‘I’ve reviewed the footage and, unfortunately, there’s nothing,’ he said sadly.

‘How can there be nothing?’ Sara asked. ‘Don’t the cameras stay on overnight?’

‘They do,’ he said, ‘but all systems have blind spots.’ He pulled up a video which had the date of the day the painting went missing on it. The area which housed the school exhibition had a single camera, which rotated around the room. Geoff put it into fast forward so we could watch the hours pass quickly. We saw all of us students come in, look around and leave. Then nothing, until Margaret and a team of staff came in and started pulling down the artworks and moving them into different groups for re-hanging. We watched Margaret take Grace's portrait down from the wall herself and lean it up against a stack of other paintings. The camera kept moving and the pile of artwork was no longer visible on the screen. Then it rotated back.

'Wait, stop there!' Grace said.

Geoff paused the footage.

'Look, my painting is now gone,' Grace said, pointing to the stack.

We all squinted.

'How can you tell? There are a whole pile of them in that stack,' Geoff said, leaning in.

'You could see my painting's frame sticking out before. And now it's gone.'

Geoff sat back and sucked in a breath. 'You're right. But there's no footage of someone taking it.'

We nodded grimly.

'Hey, wait, look!' Sara said, peering at the screen.

On the far right, at the very edge of the camera view, was an arm.

'That could be anyone's arm,' Geoff said, shrugging.

'No, look,' Sara insisted, pointing at the sleeve, which looked like a rugby jersey with a stripe down the arm.

'That looks like the Crestwood Hall rugby jumper,' Archie said.

'Kai,' Sara whispered.

We all nodded.

'We need to confront him again as soon as we get back to school,' I said resolutely.

Geoff turned the video off and apologised that he didn't have any other information to report on the missing painting.

We decided to keep looking around the gallery for more clues, while we waited for Mrs Hodges. Since we didn't have Margaret with us, we couldn't look in any of the restricted areas. But we wandered around the rest of the gallery, stopping to ask the different staff questions. After an hour of this, we felt no closer to finding Grace's artwork than when we'd arrived.

'This really should be the job of the police,' Grace said finally, frustrated.

'I doubt the police think this is a big enough deal to bother with,' Archie said sadly.

Feeling dejected (which means sad and depressed), we headed back to the interschool competition exhibit. But as we entered, we saw a tall figure staring at a painting. It was Kai. He was wearing his rugby jersey and had his sports bag flung over his shoulder.

'Looks like we don't need to wait to go back to school to see Kai,' Sara said, pointing. 'Look who's here!'

'Why does he need a sports bag in an art gallery?' Archie whispered suspiciously.

'I think it's time for the confrontation,' Sara said.

Archie opened his mouth to protest, but before he could, we three girls were already marching over to Kai.

'OK, Kai, it's time to come clean,' Sara said in her most confident voice. 'How did you know Grace's artwork was missing before we'd told anyone?'

Kai shook his head. 'Not you losers again. Can't you just leave me alone?'

'How'd you know?' Grace demanded.

'Lottie told me,' he said. 'She was in the gym on the treadmill when I was doing weights training at lunch yesterday.'

We all quietened. Lottie could well have told him about the missing painting.

'Well, what were you doing at the gallery by yourself?' Sara spat.

Kai's cheeks reddened.

At that moment, Archie lunged forward and grabbed Kai's sports bag.

'Yeah, well what's THIS?' Archie yelled, pulling at a rolled-up poster that was sticking out the end of the bag.

'Don't you dare open that!' Kai yelled.

'Is it my painting?' Grace shrieked.

Archie unrolled the poster and then froze.

'Give me that!' Kai said, snatching the poster back.

'It's for the Cathedral Choir,' Archie said, confused. 'Why do you have a poster for the Cathedral Choir?'

Kai breathed in deeply, his mind clearly racing for an explanation. But then he exhaled and shook his head.

'If you dweebs tell anyone about this, your lives won't be worth living, OK?' he said in a low voice.

We all nodded, confused.

He opened the poster, and, sure enough, it was an ad for an upcoming concert by the Cathedral Choir. It showed a photo of boys of all ages in white robes, singing in the big cathedral in the middle of London. But our mouths fell open when we saw the soloist at the front.

It was Kai! He was wearing a long white gown and his spiky hair had been parted and brushed down to the side. His mouth was open in song and he looked, well, angelic.

'You're in the Cathedral Choir?' Archie asked, shocked.

'Yes. That's where I was the other day. I go to the evening mass with Ms Saunders, the music teacher. That's why I was unaccompanied in the logbook. The office staff know I go with her, so they never worry about filling it out. But you'd better not tell *anyone* about this.'

'Why not? Singing is great,' I said.

'It's just . . . it's not something my rugby friends

would expect me to do,' Kai said slowly. 'And, you know, wearing the gown . . .' his voice trailed off.

'If they were really your friends, they wouldn't care that you sing,' Archie said.

'I don't care,' Kai said angrily. 'You're *not* to tell anyone!'

'OK, OK,' Archie said, raising his hands in a calming motion.

'But what about the rugby sleeve we saw on the security footage?' I asked, thinking of Geoff's video.

'There are a few Senior rugby guys and girls in the art competition,' Kai said simply. 'Callum and Andrea mentioned they'd been back to the gallery.'

I nodded. Even if there were Seniors at the gallery, they wouldn't be on our suspects list because they didn't have anything to gain from stealing Grace's work—they were in a different age division.

'Look, I've gotta go. Ms Saunders is waiting to take me to choir practice now. I just thought I'd drop in and check out the art show now it was up properly. But I mean it, you better keep your mouths shut,' Kai said.

'Of course,' Archie said quietly.

Kai offered a small smile and nodded lightly at Archie, then turned and walked towards the exit.

'Wow,' Archie breathed when Kai had gone. 'Who knew?!'

'I can't quite believe it myself,' Sara said, shaking her head. 'Kai—a choir boy!'

'But this totally ruins our theory,' Grace said sadly. 'Kai has an alibi, so now we have no idea who has taken my artwork. And the judging is in four days.'

Suddenly, a voice came over the loudspeaker of the gallery.

'Attention, patrons. There has been a security breach. We are temporarily locking down the gallery. Please gather in the main lobby, where you can exit after a brief search by the police.'

We looked at other, confused and alarmed. Members of the public began to flock to the lobby, some lightly jogging with worried expressions on their faces. Geoff and the other security staff were calmly guarding the closed entrance doors, while constantly reassuring people that they were in no danger.

Margaret shuffled over to us. 'Children, where's your teacher? Come stand over here with me,' she said, puffing lightly.

'What's going on?' Grace asked.

'There's been a security breach. But you are not in any danger. I'll just wait with you until your teacher finds you,' she said.

Suddenly the big entrance doors opened, and we watched multiple policemen pile into the gallery. They began to order everyone into a line and started inspecting bags as people exited the building one by one.

'What is going on?' Archie cried.

'Well, I shouldn't really be giving you this information, but . . .' Margaret's voice trailed off.

'What is it? A wild animal? A bomb?' Sara asked, panic rising in her voice.

Margaret shook her head. 'Oh no, nothing like that. It's that valuable painting—*The Holy Cherubim* . . .'

'The 16-million-dollar one?' Archie asked.

Margaret nodded. 'It's . . . well . . . it's gone.'

Chapter 11

× –

From: Ella

Sent: Sunday, 10:05 AM (UTC+01:00) London

To: Olivia

Subject: A real life mystery!

Hi Olivia,

Well, you'll never believe what has been happening over here in London. First, Grace's portrait disappeared from the competition exhibition. She is positively disconsolate, which means nothing is giving her any comfort. But then, can you believe, a 16-million-dollar painting ALSO went missing from the same gallery! The police came straight away and the gallery had to close, although they didn't come when Grace's painting went missing, which I think is RUDE! They are completely baffled (which means confused) as to how that painting could have just walked out of the gallery without anyone noticing or setting off any alarms. It's like it disappeared into thin air—POUFF!

So now we have two mysteries to solve. Could they be linked? But why would someone steal a 16-million-dollar painting *and* a kid's piece of art? No offence to Grace—her art is amazing—but I don't think it's worth any money. What would a thief do with a painting of Grace's brother?!

It's like a real-life *Millie Mysteries* book. We are determined to get to the bottom of it, so that Grace's painting can still be judged in the art competition. And also to solve the bigger mystery of the valuable missing painting. Imagine if we found it! We'd be heroes! We'd probably get to meet the Queen and she would give us medals and maybe even knight us!

I'm going to do some more brainstorming with Sara, Grace and Archie. If the gallery is open again today, we might be able to go and interview Margaret about the missing painting. It'd make a great story for Eden Press!

Chat to you later!

Love, Ella

x

Archie, Sara, Grace and I bundled out of the Tube station, Lottie trailing behind us with her friend, Bethany, who had agreed to come too. Even though they were supposed to be our chaperones while we were at the gallery, I was pretty sure they were going to ditch us the minute we arrived and go and sit in the gallery café on their phones.

The gallery had stayed closed all day Sunday and Monday, but we'd heard that it would be open to the public again on Tuesday, despite the ongoing investigations into the missing artwork. Still, I breathed a sigh of relief when we arrived and saw that the gallery was indeed open, although I noticed there were security guards all around the outside of the building now.

We entered and scanned our passes, saying hi to Geoff as we walked in. Inside, I could see an even heavier presence of police and security. It gave the gallery a strange prison-like feeling rather than the free artistic feeling it'd had before.

A policeman eyed each one of us carefully as we walked past, so Sara stopped and cleared her throat. 'Excuse me, sir,' she said.

The policeman looked down at her and adjusted his hat slightly.

'I'm sure you are busy with *The Holy Cherubim* missing painting, but I was wondering if you had any information on whether or not the other missing artwork had been found.'

The policeman's eyes widened. 'What do you mean?' he asked, alarmed.

'Well, my friend here, Grace, had her painting stolen too, from the exhibit just over there,' Sara said, pointing first to Grace, who waved shyly, and then to the interschool competition exhibition hall.

The policeman exhaled, clearly relieved. 'Oh, I thought you meant another *real* artwork had been stolen!' He laughed. 'You really had me going for a moment there!'

Grace frowned.

'It *is* a real artwork,' I said defensively. 'Grace's piece won a place in this international art competition. It's inspired by Picasso, you know.'

The policeman laughed even louder. 'OK, OK, I see. I'll tell you what, kids,' he said.

I didn't like the way he said 'kids'.

'I'll keep an eye out for your craft, OK?'

The word that jumped into my head was patronising. That's when someone speaks to you like you are a complete baby, like you have no idea what you're talking about. It made me annoyed.

'Come on, guys,' Archie said. 'We'll have to find it ourselves.'

As we walked away, we could hear the policeman

calling over his colleagues to tell them what we'd said. They all started laughing.

At that point, Margaret came shuffling over.

'Oh, you're back! I'm so glad. I was worried you might have had a terrible fright the other day,' she said, smiling at each of us.

'We tried to ask the policeman about Grace's missing artwork, but he just laughed at us,' Sara said huffily.

'That's a bit patronising, isn't it?' Margaret said. I beamed at her for using the very word I'd just thought of myself.

'I guess it shows we need to keep looking ourselves,' Grace said quietly. 'But I'm losing hope, Margaret. The judges are coming to look at the exhibition tomorrow.'

Margaret stroked Grace's arm. 'It can't have vanished,' she said soothingly.

'But it kind of appears as if it has. Along with *The Holy Cherubim*,' I said. 'Margaret, do you have any more information on the robbery?'

Margaret's eyes twinkled as if she held a secret.

'Please tell us!' I begged.

She burst into a smile. 'Look, I don't have much, but let's go sit down and we'll have a chat about what I know.'

'And who knows, it might even lead us to Grace's work, too!' I said excitedly.

We walked over to a set of leather seats in the main hallway of the gallery. As we sat down, I opened my notebook and clicked my pen to extend the tip.

'So, have there been any developments?' I asked.

Margaret shook her head. 'No leads yet. The police are baffled.'

'How could a thief have stolen the artwork? Aren't there cameras everywhere? And what about alarms?' Grace asked.

'That's the most baffling bit,' Margaret said. 'As I explained to you before, all the works are microchipped. When the artwork left the building, alarms should have sounded. But they didn't. That tells us the thief must have removed the microchip.'

'And what about the cameras?' I asked, scribbling down more notes.

Margaret hesitated. 'Well, I suppose not every single corner of the gallery has a camera.'

'Then the thief must have known where the blind spots in the gallery are!' Archie said excitedly.

'An inside job?' Sara suggested.

Margaret looked a little panicked.

'Now, wait there, hold your horses,' Margaret said, her voice shaking slightly. 'I don't want you young things running around accusing the gallery staff. That isn't fair.'

Margaret was right. Innocent until proven guilty.

'I'm happy to help you with your report, but I want you to promise that you will only talk to me about this. I could get into a lot of trouble for helping you, and if you run around accusing people, it'll be obvious I've been sharing information with you. So, this stays between us, OK?' Margaret said with serious eyes.

We all nodded.

'We promise,' Sara said.

Margaret relaxed slightly.

'Margaret!' a voice called from across the lobby.

It was Geoff, the security guard. He jogged over to us.

'There's something I think you and the kids will want to see!' he said excitedly. 'Follow me!'

We went over to the 'Staff Only' access door, and Geoff scanned his pass and ushered us all into the concrete stairwell. We followed him down multiple flights of stairs, Margaret puffing along behind us. When we got to the bottom floor, we exited into a cold concrete hallway.

'Where are we?' Archie asked, shivering slightly.

'This is the gallery storage area. We keep all the boring things down here, like cleaning equipment, spare frames, curtains and exhibition decorations,' Margaret said.

'Where's that cold wind coming from?' Sara asked.

'The loading bay is down here, too. This is where the trucks deliver artwork and supplies to the gallery and take away shipments and rubbish,' Geoff said. 'But that's not what I want to show you. Come on!'

He hurried into a light jog, and we followed him up the hallway. Then he stopped in front of a grey door labelled 'Storage' and scanned his pass. We heard the lock *beep* and the door opened with a clunk.

'I was down here putting away some old security equipment and look what I found!'

Geoff swung open the door and turned on the light. Old mannequins missing arms and legs and long velvet curtains were bundled up on the floor. There were mops and buckets and cleaning products on the shelves. Margaret was right, it did all look rather boring. But as we walked in, I heard Grace shriek.

'It's here!' she yelled.

Grace ran over to where a bunch of brooms were standing up against a wall, and there, behind the brooms, was a flash of colour. She moved the brooms to the side and pulled out her artwork.

'Your art!' Archie squealed, as he ran over and hugged Grace.

'How on earth did it get down here?' Margaret asked.

'No idea,' said Geoff. 'But here it is!'

'Oh, thank you!' Grace said, hugging Geoff quickly, then turning back to her art. 'I can't believe we've found it—and just in time for the judging tomorrow!'

'Is it damaged at all?' Sara asked, leaning in closer to see.

Grace inspected every corner and detail of her piece, then smiled widely. 'It's perfect.'

I looked at the artwork, then cocked my head to the side. 'Is something different?' I asked, leaning in as well. I couldn't put my finger on it.

Grace scanned her eyes over the portrait again. 'No, it's exactly the same,' she said.

I shrugged. I must have been mistaken. Grace would know her own artwork better than I did.

'Let's get this back up to the gallery,' Margaret said excitedly.

As Grace carried the painting out of the storeroom, Geoff laughed to himself. 'Now if only *The Holy Cherubim* would just turn up behind a broom!' he chuckled.

Margaret laughed. 'Wouldn't that be something?'

Chapter 12

When I was younger, my Nanna Kate always told me that she had eyes in the back of her head. I remember trying to sneak looks at her nest of curly hair to see if there really were eyes in there. She did always seem to know when we were up to mischief, even when she wasn't looking at us.

I remember this one time, I dared Olivia to sneak some cookies from Nanna Kate's pantry while she was in the living room watching TV. Olivia crawled past on all fours, so she was hidden by the back of the couch. Then, when she got to the kitchen, she tiptoed over to the pantry and opened it without a sound. But just as she was reaching for the cookie jar, Nanna Kate said, 'I wouldn't do that if I were you!' She completely startled Olivia, who sent the whole jar of cookies showering down around her. My brother, Max, and I were hiding in the hallway, and had kept our eyes on Nanna Kate the whole time. She'd never even turned around once. We couldn't believe it. It was only years later, when I was sitting in Nanna Kate's lounge myself, that I noticed you could see the reflection of the kitchen in the big mirror on the wall of the lounge room. I realised Nanna Kate didn't have eyes in the back of her head at all—she just knew where to look in her own house.

I sat bolt upright in my bed, suddenly awake.

That's it! I thought to myself.

I looked around the dark dorm room. Tiny slivers of light from the moon shone through the curtains, which were slightly ajar. I swung my feet out of bed, and the foldaway made a squeaking noise. Grace stirred in the bed opposite me.

'Ella?' she whispered.

'Grace, I've had a thought!' I said, standing up and shuffling over to her. I sat on the end of her bed, and she sleepily rubbed her eyes.

'You had a thought in the middle of the night?' she asked.

'Yes, I was thinking about the missing painting at the gallery,' I whispered. 'And then I had a crazy thought, and I can't get back to sleep because it's rattling around in my brain.'

'What's going on?' a voice in the bed next to us asked quietly. It was Sara.

'Ella's had an idea,' Grace yawned.

'And I can't sleep until I've talked about it,' I added.

Sara sat up and flung her covers off. Then she tiptoed over to Grace's bed and sat next to me.

'But we found Grace's painting,' she said, brushing her hair out of her face. 'What's left to think about?'

'The Holy Cherubim painting,' I whispered excitedly. 'It's a real-life mystery! We can't just forget about it.'

'Yes, we can,' Grace muttered, lying back down.

I shook her shoulders. 'No, we can't! Imagine the story this would be if we solved it! I could report on it for Eden Press. And it would probably make world news! We may even get to meet the Queen!'

Grace propped herself up on her elbows and raised an eyebrow in disbelief.

'Can't this brainwave wait until tomorrow?' she said.

I shook my head adamantly. Nanna Kate always said I was too stubborn for my own good.

'OK, so what were you thinking then?' Sara asked.

'I was thinking about what Margaret said earlier,' I said, standing up and tiptoeing over to my bag. I pulled out my notebook, pen and a tiny book light. Then I went back over to Grace's bed and turned the little light on, illuminating the page. 'See here,' I said, pointing to my notes. 'Margaret said it was baffling how anyone could have taken the painting, because it was microchipped and there are cameras everywhere, right? But isn't it strange how the cameras caught nothing?'

'Yeah, but she also mentioned the gallery cameras

have blind spots,' Sara whispered.

I nodded excitedly.

'I know, and that's what made me remember something I saw on Archie's phone. It could be just the clue we are looking for! We need to check it out,' I said.

'Sure, we'll check it in the morning,' Grace said, waving her hand dismissively.

'No, it's has to be now! I won't be able to sleep again until I know!'

'But we are not supposed to leave the dorm at night, you know that!' Grace said.

Usually, I would be hesitant about breaking the rules and it would be Grace trying to convince *me* to do something crazy. But this time, I felt like I was onto something massive. I needed answers. Now.

'I know,' I replied seriously.

Grace and Sara exchanged glances.

'I know where Archie's bed is,' Sara murmured. 'It's right by the window of his dorm. We could sneak out and try wake him.'

I clapped my hands silently.

'Oh, OK then,' Grace sighed, swinging her legs out of bed.

We put jumpers on over our pyjamas and slipped sneakers onto our feet. Then we crept up the centre of the dorm room, trying not to wake the other girls lying quietly sleeping.

The hallway was dark and cool. We shuffled up the carpet, being careful to keep close to the walls, in the shadows.

'What would happen if we got caught?' I whispered to Sara.

'I don't know. Detention? Suspension?'

'Deportation?' Grace asked, smirking.

I gulped.

'The stairs creak terribly here,' Sara said quietly, pointing to the cascading stairwell. 'That's the downside to living in a building a couple of hundred years old.'

'Which way then?' Grace said.

Sara lifted her leg and swung it over the wooden banister. Then she lay down on her tummy and gripped the railing with her hands. 'This way!' she smiled.

Sara pushed herself gently and went flying backwards down the banister, curling past the flights of stairs with ease. Grace's eyes went wide with delight. She jumped on after Sara and pushed off fast. I watched as she curled around the banister all the way to the ground floor, where she landed on the marble with a light thud.

'Now or never,' I whispered to myself, and jumped on. I pushed off and felt myself whooshing backwards down the smooth wooden railing. I couldn't see behind me and suddenly realised I wouldn't be able to tell where the stairs ended. Just as I had that thought, I found myself falling off the end of the banister and landing on top of Grace, who was still sitting on the floor.

'Oof!'

'Sorry, Grace!' I whispered. Sara giggled.

We stood up and crept over to the dorm's front doors. But Sara walked past them to a nearby window.

'The doors will be locked, but we can get out the

windows easily,' she whispered.

'Why do I get the feeling you've done this before?' I asked suspiciously.

Sara just smiled mischievously, and gently turned the lock of the window and slid it to the side. One by one, we climbed out into the flowerbed beneath. I looked up and saw the night was clear, with a brilliant moon hanging like a chandelier in the sky. The summer evening was cooler than I had expected, and I shivered lightly, glad for my jumper.

'Where to now?' I asked, excitement pulsing through my body.

'This way,' Sara said, beckoning us to follow her across the damp lawn.

We shuffled over to the opposite building, where the boys' dorms were.

'Archie's bed is right by that window,' Sara said, pointing upwards.

She bent down to pick up a small pebble and threw it towards his window. It bounced lightly off the glass, making a clacking sound.

We waited.

Nothing.

Then she tried again.

Still nothing.

'Let me try,' Grace said, pushing Sara to the side. She picked up a rock and, before we could stop her, hurled it towards Archie's window. Luckily, she missed the glass, but it made a loud clanging noise as it bounced off the metal drainpipe.

'Grace!' Sara groaned.

But a second later we could see Archie's face looking out the window.

Grace smiled smugly.

'What are you doing?' he hissed, as he opened the window.

'I need to see your phone!' I shout-whispered.

'What?!' Archie said, disbelieving. 'In the middle of the night?!'

'Ella has a hunch,' Grace said. 'And when Ella has a hunch, there's no stopping her.'

Archie shook his head and disappeared back into

his room. A couple of minutes later, we saw him slide open the downstairs window near the boys' dorm entrance, just like we had done at our dorm. He jogged over to us and we all huddled together, making sure we were standing in the shadow of the building and not the bright moonlight.

'Here. What do you want?' he asked, pulling his phone out of his pocket.

'Can I see your photos of us at the gallery's Renaissance exhibit the other day?' I asked.

He nodded and opened his photos app, swiping through various photos of the artworks and some selfies of us around London and in the art gallery itself.

'There, stop!' I said, taking Archie's phone and pulling it closer to my face. I pinched my fingers together and then opened them to zoom in on the background of one of the photos. 'I knew this was what I had seen!' I breathed.

'What is it?' Grace said, peering over my shoulder.

'Remember what Margaret said about the cameras having blind spots?' I asked.

Everyone nodded.

'And how when *The Holy Cherubim* was stolen, the thief somehow managed to avoid all of the cameras?'

My friends nodded again.

'But that makes no sense, because there would never have been a blind spot over the most valuable painting in the building, right? So how on earth did they get it off the wall without being seen?' I said, getting more and more excited.

Archie cocked his head to the side. 'Yeah, that is weird,' he said.

'Then I suddenly remembered this,' I said, turning the phone around to show them. It was a selfie of us standing in the room where *The Holy Cherubim* was hanging. We were all smiling at the camera, and even Margaret had come in on the selfie. 'Look closely,' I said, as I zoomed in.

'Is that . . .' Sara said.

'. . . Geoff?' Grace finished.

In the background of our selfie was our security guard friend, Geoff. He was looking slightly sideways and had his hand on the security camera on the wall behind us. And the camera was turned to face the wall.

'Did Geoff move the camera?' Archie asked.

'Sara was right—it's an inside job!' I said. 'The only way someone could possibly get away with this robbery was to have someone on the inside who knows all about the gallery.'

'And who better than a security guard?' Sara whispered.

'But Geoff is our friend,' Archie said quietly.

'He found my artwork,' Grace added.

We all stood in silence. I shivered in the light wind.

Suddenly, an artificial light flickered on across the pathway.

'Hide!' Sara hissed.

We jumped into the flowerbed and hid behind a hedge, just as one of the Crestwood security guards wandered up the path towards the boys' dorms. We all held our breath as he walked right past us, thankful that he didn't shine his torch in our direction. But as he got to the front door of the boys' dorm, he stopped. I could see him frown in the light reflecting on his face. He walked over to the window and shone his torch on it.

'Oh no,' Archie said, clapping his hand to his forehead.

The security guard looked around, shrugged and slid the window shut. We all heard the internal lock click shut. Then the guard continued on up the path and through the archway towards the front of the school.

'Thanks a lot, now I'm locked out!' Archie hissed.

'Well, there's one window still open,' Grace said, looking up. The window to Archie's room hung open from when he had leant out it to talk to us. But it was two storeys up.

Grace tapped the drainpipe and raised her eyebrows. 'Are you a good climber?' she asked.

Archie groaned.

We gave him a boost and he slowly started shimmying up the drainpipe, using the brackets to help push himself up with his feet. I could see his skinny arms trembling as he tried to hoist his body up the pipe.

'You'd better not be looking,' he said self-consciously,

adjusting his pyjama shorts with one hand.

We giggled and moved back so we weren't standing underneath Archie.

'You're nearly there!' Sara said.

Archie made it to his level, but then he had to get from the drainpipe to his window. I was suddenly overcome with a feeling of dread—if Archie fell he could be really badly hurt.

'Maybe this wasn't the best idea?' I said hesitantly.

Archie stretched out one leg and just managed to get his foot on the windowsill. But the other foot was still on the drainpipe.

'I'm stuck!' he hissed, frozen in a starfish shape between the drainpipe and the window.

'On the count of three, you need to push yourself off the drainpipe and grab the window with both hands,' Grace said.

I closed my eyes.

'One. Two. Three!'

Archie pushed off the drainpipe and grabbed for the window. His body swayed and he almost fell, but he was able to grab hold and pull himself onto the thick window ledge.

Grace, Sara and I let out a big sigh of relief.

Archie hoisted himself inside the window and then stuck his head back out.

'Made it!' he whispered, fist pumping the air.

'We'd better get back,' Sara said. 'That's enough excitement for one night.'

Grace and I nodded, waved to Archie and followed Sara back to our dorm. But as we tiptoed along, I couldn't stop thinking about the image I'd seen on Archie's phone. Why *was* Geoff touching the security camera? And could he really be involved in one of the biggest robberies London had ever seen?

Chapter 13

Mrs Hodges was beaming with pride as she led the Eden girls through the entrance to the art gallery. There was a large crowd inside, with groups from schools all over the United Kingdom, including England, Scotland, Wales and Northern Ireland. And, of course, Eden College. Gallery staff were showing adults in suits into the 'International Student Portrait Prize' exhibition, where Grace's art would once again be hanging proudly on the wall.

We walked through the security checkpoint and Geoff waved to us excitedly. 'Good luck, Grace and

Archie!' he called. 'I hope you both win!'

Archie and I exchanged glances. Could Geoff *really* be involved in the art robbery?

Dr Smythe, the Headmistress of Crestwood Hall, was also in the gallery, smiling widely. She walked over to us and gave Archie's arm a light squeeze. 'Good luck, Archie,' she said. 'You are doing all of us at Crestwood Hall so proud.'

Archie blushed. 'I'm probably not going to win, you know,' he said shyly.

'We're just proud you got this far!' Dr Smythe exclaimed. 'It is a big achievement!'

Archie shrugged, unconvinced.

Margaret bustled up to us, holding out her arms. 'You're here!' She was wearing what I presumed to be one of her best dresses. She had a little more make-up on than normal and her grey curly hair was pinned back with a bobby pin. She wore a pretty flowery brooch on her cardigan and around her neck hung her staff pass.

'How are you feeling, Grace and Archie?' she

gushed, clasping her hands together like a proud grandmother.

'A little nervous,' Grace admitted.

Before she could say anything else, we were called into the exhibition hall along with the other schools. The room looked even more magical than usual. The banner we'd made had been strung up on the back wall above a small podium, and fairy lights framed the walls where the artwork hung. Students in various school uniforms walked around, eyeing their competition.

Three adults—two women and one man—were walking around with clipboards. They all wore suit jackets and looked very serious. Each one leaned in close to the portrait they were looking at, squinting in concentration.

'I bet they are the judges,' Sara whispered, pointing to them.

We all nodded.

Grace kept her eyes on one particular judge, who was standing in front of her painting. He frowned and tilted his head to the side. He leant in close, then stepped back. He frowned again, squinted, then briefly nodded before writing something down on his clipboard.

'I can't tell if he loves it or hates it,' she said, jittering up and down nervously.

I glanced over to the other side of the room and saw Kai standing in front of his artwork, his hands on his hips, beaming proudly. He caught my eye and nervously adjusted his posture.

We mingled around for ages, while the judges evaluated each portrait. Then we were all called together for the announcement of the winners. The competitors stood at the front of the room, and the head judge stepped up to the lectern microphone, which had been set up on the podium against the far wall.

'Thank you, everyone, for an amazing international art show,' he beamed. 'And a special thank you to our friends from Eden College, who have travelled across the world to be here with us today.'

Everyone applauded politely and the Eden College artists up the front smiled proudly.

'I'm going to invite Ms Caroline Drewry, the Head of Exhibitions here at the gallery, to come and announce the winners.'

A woman with a bright smiled stepped up to the microphone.

'We will begin with our youngest category—the under 13s,' she said.

I gave Grace a little wave from where I was standing. Sara made a fist and mouthed, 'You've got this!' to Archie.

'Highly commended awards go to . . .' Ms Drewry listed two names from schools I didn't know, then announced, '. . . and Grace from Eden College.'

I squealed.

Grace looked completely shocked. She walked up to the judges and shook hands with them as they presented her with a ribbon.

'Yay, Grace!' Sara cheered.

Out of all the entrants from all over the world, Grace had been highly commended. I scribbled down the names in my notebook for my Eden Press article and took a stack of photos of Grace standing up the front with her ribbon.

'The runner-up is Emily from Barrington College,' Ms Drewry announced.

We all applauded.

'And in first place, Archie from Crestwood Hall!'

Archie's jaw fell open, as he stood frozen to the spot. Sara and I looked at each other with wide eyes, before cheering madly.

'Go get your award, Archie,' Margaret urged from behind us.

Archie shook his head and walked up to the judges, who presented him with a shining trophy.

As Archie walked back to his place, he passed Kai, who extended his arm. Archie flinched. But then he realised Kai was extending his hand for a handshake.

'Good job, Archie,' he smiled.

Archie took Kai's hand. Then he continued to his spot at the front and smiled widely as the crowd cheered.

'Oh, I'm so happy for Archie,' Sara beamed. 'He told

me he's never won *anything* before.'

The Head of Exhibitions continued announcing the awards, right up to the final category for the oldest students. By the end, we realised Grace and Archie were the only prize winners from Eden College and Crestwood Hall. When they stepped back into the crowd, they were engulfed by students and teachers, all of whom were eager to offer their congratulations. Dr Smythe and Mrs Hodges stood proudly for a photo with both Archie and Grace. The professional photographer took a dozen photos, his flash blinding us as we stood watching from the side.

When they finally made their way over to us, we enveloped them both in a group hug.

'Highly commended—that's amazing, Grace!' Sara beamed.

'And first place to Archie,' Grace said, turning the attention to him. 'Congratulations!'

Archie's cheeks coloured pink. 'I never thought I would win,' he said quietly.

'You deserve it,' I said, giving him another hug.

When I pulled back from him, his face glowed bright red. Suddenly, my own cheeks flushed pink.

'Can I get a photo of you two?' I asked hurriedly, gesturing for Grace and Archie to stand together with their awards. I clicked my camera on my phone as the two of them stood grinning proudly.

'And one in front of your artworks,' I said.

We walked over to Grace's portrait. An additional ribbon had been placed on the silver frame, saying 'Highly Commended'. Grace stood in front and beamed while I took a picture. I looked at the shot on my phone to check it was clear and paused. I had that feeling again that something had changed in Grace's piece. I zoomed in. But . . . no, it was the same. I must have just been confused.

After I took a photo of Archie in front of his winning piece, we gathered together outside the exhibit room.

Archie let out a loud sigh. 'I don't know about you, Grace, but I think I need a break from all this attention,' he said. I got the feeling Archie wasn't used to being fawned over.

'So, what do you want to do?' Sara asked.

'Let's get back to the mystery. We need to find out more about Geoff,' Archie said. 'We need to know why he was fiddling with the security camera that day.'

'Yeah, but we can't just walk up to him and accuse him,' Grace said.

'Let's go tell him our news, and then maybe we can bring it up in conversation somehow,' I suggested.

Archie shrugged, but the others nodded.

We found Geoff sitting by the security entrance. The computer screens with camera footage of all the rooms in the gallery blinked in front of him.

'Archie won!' Grace yelled to him, as we walked over.

Geoff's eyes came to life. 'Archie, my boy! Great job!' He reached out to give Archie an enthusiastic high-five.

'And Grace got highly commended,' Archie added.

Geoff beamed and patted Grace happily on the back. 'I'm in the presence of *two* famous artists! How lucky am I?!' he smiled.

'So, how's the surveillance going?' Archie asked, moving around to Geoff's side of the table.

'Not much to report,' Geoff said, shrugging.

'I see there's a camera in the main gallery where *The Holy Cherubim* was last seen,' Grace said lightly. She pointed to a screen, which clearly showed the place where the painting had last been hanging. I glanced at Geoff. His cheeks looked warm.

'Ah, yep,' he said. His forehead glistened with just a little bit of sweat.

'It's a bit odd, isn't it?' Archie said, leaning in. 'Why didn't the camera catch the robbery?'

Geoff began to stammer. 'Oh . . . ah, well, sometimes they aren't always pointing in the right direction,' he mumbled.

'But it was pointing at the painting when we were in there,' I said casually. 'I remember thinking it was watching us.'

'It's almost like someone . . . moved it,' Sara said.

Geoff looked at us wildly, then his shoulders sagged. 'What do you kids know?' he whispered.

I looked at my friends. Should we tell Geoff? If he was a criminal, he might be dangerous. But what if there was a perfectly reasonable explanation?

Sara nodded at me.

'We have a photo of us in front of the painting that was stolen,' I said slowly, and gestured for Archie to show him the photo.

Archie held up his phone as he zoomed in on the photo's background. And there was Geoff, adjusting the camera.

'Oh dear,' Geoff said sadly.

'Why were you tampering with the camera?' Sara asked quietly.

Geoff looked up, alarmed. 'You kids don't think I had something to do with the robbery, do you?' He looked hurt.

'No, of course not! We just . . . well, we thought . . .' My voice trailed off. Our betrayal hung heavy and silent in the air.

'I suppose it does look suspicious,' Geoff said. 'The truth is, I was cleaning the camera. Honestly—look more closely at the photo. You can see the rag in my hand.'

'Why didn't you just say so?' Archie asked.

'Because I stuffed up. I didn't notice I'd moved the camera when I was cleaning it, because I was trying to keep an eye on you kids. That camera should have been looking straight at *The Holy Cherubim*. If anyone knows it was me that adjusted it, I could lose my job.' Geoff looked at us with pleading eyes. 'I may not have stolen the painting, but I know this is my fault.'

We all looked at each other with sympathetic expressions. Was Geoff's story true?

I glanced back at him and saw his eyes were glistening with tears. 'We won't tell anyone,' I said quickly.

'The police are bound to find out sooner or later, so I should come clean,' Geoff said, shrugging. 'I guess I just hoped I wouldn't get into trouble.'

Archie patted him on the arm. 'It's OK, Geoff. We believe you.'

Geoff smiled gratefully.

'I'd better get back to work,' Geoff said, turning to the monitor. 'We can't have another crime happening on my watch.'

We said goodbye and walked back over to the exhibition room.

'Do you believe him?' Sara asked.

'He looked so genuine,' I said.

'But it's a bit convenient,' Grace said doubtfully.

'Well, let's just keep an eye on him,' Archie said. 'It would make a lot of sense if he was involved—he knows more about this place than anyone else here.'

I jotted down our findings in my notebook, then flipped it closed. We had a motive. We had a suspect. And we had a theory. But something told me that it wasn't Geoff at all. I didn't really know why, but what I did know was that we needed to keep digging.

Chapter 14

X —

From: Ella

Sent: Saturday, 9:07 AM (UTC+01:00) London

To: Olivia

Subject: Dead ends

Hi Olivia,

I hope your presentation on Ancient Egypt went well. Did you end up making the mask and doing your whole speech in it? That would have been so funny.

Things in London are good. It's been several days since the big competition announcement at the art gallery.

Grace and Archie came back to Crestwood Hall like heroes—everyone was cheering for them and asking to see their awards! Archie said he can't believe it—now everyone knows his name and even that bully Kai is being nice to him.

And guess what we got to do yesterday? We went to *Enchantment the Musical* in the West End! Tilly and I couldn't believe it. It was just like our school musical, but even more fabulous. I wish you'd been there to see it too! It even took my mind off that mystery we've been trying to solve.

The Holy Cherubim painting still hasn't been found. Margaret at the gallery says that the police are at a dead end. And even though I really wanted to solve the mystery for Eden Press (and so we could meet the Queen), we haven't been able to make any new discoveries either. I still don't think Geoff the security guard was involved, even though he has access to all the gallery information. Sara says that just because someone seems like your friend doesn't mean they are innocent. But something in my gut tells me Geoff isn't the culprit.

I wish I had other leads to follow, but I just don't.

So, I think we might have to call it quits on our investigation, which makes me feel sad. It's like a *Millie Mysteries* book without a proper ending. But we don't have much more time in London, and we won't be visiting the gallery again, except to say goodbye to Margaret and Geoff. The exhibit has been packed up and Grace's art will be shipped back to Australia today.

Better go. We are off to see some markets this morning and I can't wait!

Love, Ella

The summer sun was shining down on us and it was the perfect day for more sightseeing in London. Lottie and her friend had agreed to accompany us into town again, and Sara and Archie decided we should check out the Portobello Road markets. As we walked the street, the first thing we were drawn to was the tantalising smell coming from a crepe stall. A woman stood in front of a big round hotplate, pouring batter onto it. Then she took up a tool that looked like a window wiper, and moved the batter around in a circle, spreading it out thinly. My mouth watered as we waited in line.

Grace ordered one with bananas and whipped cream, Archie and Sara got strawberries and cream on theirs and I got chocolate hazelnut spread. Even though Lottie and her friend were meant to stay with us the whole time, they had already disappeared into a vintage clothes shop after vowing to meet us outside in 30 minutes.

'This crepe is amazing,' Grace said, closing her eyes as she took another bite of her thin rolled-up pancake.

We all nodded our approval, as we stuffed more into our mouths. The sweet, nutty chocolate flavour spread out around my tongue, and I immediately thought about how much Olivia would love it.

As we walked up the street, I suddenly felt a pang of homesickness as I realised that my Nanna Kate would love this antiques market. There were old pieces of furniture, wooden toys, vintage clothes and beautiful jewellery in the shops and stalls lining the road. I bought Mum a pretty necklace and Max a little teddy bear wearing an English beefeater costume. Then I bought a ring with a bright blue stone for Olivia and a beautiful wooden cheese block for Dad, tucking it all in my backpack. I just needed to find something for Nanna Kate.

We continued walking up the cobbled street, stopping to look at interesting bits and pieces as we went. Then, up ahead, we saw a small crowd gathering and decided to check out what was going on. In the middle of the path was a man wearing a silver costume with silver paint from head to toe, which made his skin sparkle in the summer sun. He looked like a tin man.

He started doing magic tricks—first making scarves appear out of thin air. He juggled them deftly (which means in a clever and talented way), the coloured pieces gently floating through the air as he snatched each one before it plummeted to the ground. He moved in smooth, fluid motions, but didn't say a word. We clapped each time he finished a trick, laughing as he made a man's watch disappear and then show up in his own pocket.

Then the silver man wheeled forward a silver box, opening it and tipping it forward so we could see inside. He came over to me and gently took my hand, beckoning for me to follow. I shrugged and went with him, while my friends cheered from the side.

He gestured for me to put my hand in the box and move it around. So I reached into the silver box and felt around the soft, black velvet lining. Then he mimed for me to pick up the box, which I did, and motioned for me to turn it upside-down. I turned the box over and nothing fell out of it onto the floor. We'd established that the box was empty.

The silver man then took the box off me, put it down and closed the lid, before handing me a wand. He gestured for me to tap it on the box, which I did lightly. He then opened the box, and I was disappointed to see there was still nothing in it.

He shook his head lightly at me and frowned. He was pretending I hadn't done the wand-waving properly.

He gestured for me to flurry the wand about before tapping it on the silver box. I copied his motions, waving the wand before tapping it on the box again.

I held my breath as the silver man bent down and reached for the box. As he opened the lid, four white doves came fluttering out and up into the clear blue sky. My mouth dropped open. How had so many birds been hiding in the box? The crowd cheered loudly, and the silver man took a bow.

'Wow, that was incredible,' Sara said, as I went back over to my friends.

'It's impossible,' I murmured, trying to work out how the trick could have been done.

'Not impossible,' Archie corrected. 'The best magic always hides things in plain sight. The skill is in keeping you from seeing it.'

I stared thoughtfully at the magician.

'What now?' Sara asked.

'I think it's time for ice cream!' Grace said, raising her eyebrows and pointing to a Mr Whippy van.

The others agreed.

'Ella?' Archie said.

I startled, snapping out of my thoughts. I'd still been staring at the silver man, who was packing up his magic show. *How did he do that last trick?*

'Oh, yes, ice cream,' I said. 'Absolutely!'

As we walked towards the ice cream truck, I kept an eye on the shops and stalls in case I saw something perfect for my Nanna Kate. Then I saw a store filled with beautiful ornate frames.

'Hold on, guys,' I said. 'Do you mind if I quickly pick a frame for my Nanna Kate? She's an artist and she'd love one of those small antique frames.'

The others nodded and we looked in the window.

'Ooh, I like that one,' Grace said, pointing to a wooden frame painted blue.

'That one looks expensive,' Sara said, pointing to a gold frame with ornate flowers on it. 'Like something out of an art gallery. Actually, it looks just like the gold frame your artwork was in, Grace.'

Grace frowned. 'My portrait was in a silver frame.'

'No, it was gold,' Sara said.

She pulled out her phone and flicked to a picture of Grace standing in front of her gold-framed artwork on the very first day we had seen it hanging in the exhibition. At the same time, Grace had pulled out her phone and scrolled to a picture I'd taken of her winning the 'Highly Commended' award after the judging of the exhibition. The frame was silver.

'I knew something about your artwork had changed,' I said, frowning. 'It was the frame!'

'Why would they change the frame?' Grace said.

All of a sudden, I felt as if the world had started spinning faster. I steadied myself on the window ledge.

'Ella, are you OK?' Archie asked.

A tumble of words from the past week washed over me.

I doubt the police think this is a big enough deal to bother with . . .

Why would someone steal a 16-million-dollar painting and *a kid's piece of art?*

What would a thief do with a painting of Grace's brother?!

'Ella?' Archie repeated.

The words echoed around my head in chaotic confusion.

An inside job?

Oh, I thought you meant another real *artwork had been stolen!*

It can't have vanished . . .

The phrases floated through my mind like puzzle pieces, slowly clicking together one by one.

When the artwork left the building, alarms should have sounded.

Just because someone seems like your friend doesn't mean they are innocent.

The best magic always hides things in plain sight. The skill is in keeping you from seeing it . . .

'Earth to Ella!' Grace yelled.

I looked at her, my mouth frozen open in shock. My friends leaned in, concerned.

I cleared my throat.

'I . . . I think I've solved the mystery.'

Chapter 15

I hurriedly explained my theory to my friends, and they listened with wide eyes.

‘That’s pretty far-fetched,’ Grace said.

‘But it also makes a tonne of sense,’ Archie added.

We stood silently, weighing up what we should do.

‘Didn’t Margaret say that the student artwork was going to be leaving the gallery today?’ Sara said.

‘Yes, she did!’ Grace exclaimed. ‘She told me to say goodbye to my painting, because it would be shipping out to Australia today at about lunchtime.’

‘What time is it now?’ Archie asked.

I looked at my watch. 'Midday. It could be leaving at any minute.'

'We need to get help,' Sara said. 'Should we call the school?'

'It's Saturday. Nobody will be at the main reception. Maybe try the boarding house number?' Archie suggested.

Sara dialled the number and waited silently. 'Nobody's picking up,' she said, concern washing over her face.

'Text Lottie and tell her to meet us at the gallery. We need to move NOW,' I said. I could hear my pulse thumping in my own ears. I knew it was a race against time.

'But do you think it could be . . . dangerous?' Archie asked hesitantly.

'We've got Margaret,' I said. 'She'll be at the gallery—she'll know what to do.'

We all agreed and hurried out of the markets.

'What's the quickest way across London?' I asked Sara and Archie.

‘Cab, for sure,’ Archie said.

We waved down one of London’s iconic black cabs and piled in.

‘Where to?’ the cabbie asked.

‘The art gallery!’ Sara exclaimed. ‘As fast as you can!’

‘Right you are!’ he said and pulled the cab out into the street.

The inside of the black cab wasn’t like the taxis at home. There was a much bigger space in the middle, and there were two double seats facing each other. The driver had his window open and the sights of London flew by.

‘How will we know if your theory is right?’ Archie asked me.

‘If we can get to the student artwork before it leaves, we’ll be able to confirm my suspicion,’ I said.

‘And do you still think it’s Geoff who is involved?’ Grace asked nervously.

We all looked at each other with sad eyes. It made the most sense. We didn’t want it to be our friend, but all the evidence pointed to him.

'If it is Geoff, I bet you he's there with the artwork to make sure it's loaded OK,' Sara said.

The cab slowed to a stop. Horns started blasting.

'What's going on?' Archie asked the cab driver.

'Traffic jam,' he growled in frustration.

We craned our necks to look ahead, and, sure enough, the traffic was in complete gridlock.

'We don't have time for this,' I said, bouncing my leg up and down nervously.

'Let's get out of here—this traffic isn't going anywhere,' Sara said. She paid the cabbie and we jumped out, looking around wildly. The cab had gotten us out of Notting Hill, but not close enough to the gallery yet—it was still too far to run. The cabs and buses were completely stationary in the line of traffic. How else could we get there *fast*?

Suddenly, we heard the sound of a horn blast in the distance.

'The Thames!' Archie shouted, and started running. 'Come on!'

We all ran after Archie, who seemed to know where he was going. We raced along streets, until we rounded a corner and saw the long winding River Thames, which snaked its way into central London.

'There's a ferry at the dock now!' Archie cried.

We bought a ticket and bolted through the gate and onto the boat, just as it readied to leave.

While the ferry wasn't as fast as a cab or bus, it was definitely faster than a cab or bus in a traffic jam. And faster than our legs, too.

We stood on the outside deck as the ferry picked up speed. The warm summer air whipped through my hair and the sun shone down from the clear blue sky. If we weren't in the middle of solving a major international mystery, I would have loved to calmly enjoy the beautiful view.

As it was, the ferry putted along the murky water as we anxiously scanned the landmarks of London to judge how close we were getting.

'Look, the London Eye!' Grace said, pointing to the large Ferris wheel we'd ridden last week.

The ferry pulled up at the next stop and Archie told us that this was where we should disembark. We ran off the ferry and up through the gates onto the footpath.

'The gallery isn't far,' Sara said, pointing. 'Let's run!'

She led the way as we bolted up the street, slowing as we tried to weave through the sudden crowd surging all over the path.

'ENGLAND!' roared a man with a red and white scarf around his neck.

'Oh, great,' Archie huffed. 'Football crowds.'

'You mean soccer?' I asked. 'In the city?'

Archie nodded. 'They'll all be going to catch the Tube to Wembley Stadium.'

Huge masses of people lurched through the streets, and they all wore white and red. Some held plastic trumpets and blew hard into them, making a cacophony of noise. *Cacophony* means loud unpleasant sounds.

'Stick together!' Sara yelled. She grabbed Grace's hand and Grace reached back to grab mine. I then turned behind me and locked eyes with Archie. I hesitated for just a moment, then grasped his hand too.

He looked down at the ground, a bit embarrassed. But there was no time for that. I quickly turned ahead and we pulled each other through the throng of people.

Finally, completely breathless, we reached the steep steps of the art gallery.

'Come on,' I cried, releasing my friends' hands and leaping up the steps two at a time.

'Slow down!' Archie said, puffing behind me.

But I couldn't slow down. We were on the verge of solving a mystery and we were almost out of time.

We burst into the gallery and ran up to the security entrance.

'Tickets, please,' an unfamiliar guard said.

We looked at each other blankly, realising we no longer had our free student exhibitor passes.

'We were participants in the international schools competition,' Grace said. 'Archie got first prize—surely we can get in.'

'That exhibition is finished, I'm afraid,' the guard said. 'You'll need to buy tickets like everyone else.'

We stepped away from the guard.

'I used all my money on the cab ride,' Sara said hopelessly.

'And mine on the ferry,' I added.

Grace and Archie shook their heads, confirming they had no money either.

I walked back up to the security guard. 'We're here to see our friends, Geoff and Margaret. They'll let us in.'

'As you can see, Geoff isn't on the doors today,' the guard said, gesturing around.

We exchanged glances with each other. Geoff had always been on the doors when we'd arrived.

'And Margaret is somewhere inside, but I'm not going looking for her,' the guard added.

We walked away from the entrance, dejected.

'OK, let's think about this logically. Where would the student artwork be leaving from?' Sara said.

'It must be that loading bay area. Remember where we were when we found Grace's artwork in that storeroom? It was on the same floor, but around the back where the trucks come in,' I said, trying to picture the layout of the gallery. 'I think it must be down there.'

I led my friends back down the steep entrance steps and around the back of the gallery.

Sure enough, there was a large gate, big enough for trucks and other vehicles to enter.

'How do we get in?' Sara asked, gesturing at the security gate and guard keeping watch right by the drive. There was no way we could sneak past him.

Right at that moment, a small van pulled up at the gate. The security guard approached the van's window and a man stuck his head out to talk to him.

'There!' Grace said, taking off.

'But—' I began to protest, only to realise the others had already followed her.

I caught up and we crept to the back of the van.

'I hope it's open,' Archie whispered.

The driver was still distracted, talking to the guard, so Sara pulled on the handle of the van's back door.

It opened.

'Get in,' she whispered.

We slithered into the van and gently shut the door behind us. Thankfully, there was a barrier between the back of the van and the driver, so he couldn't see in to where we were. There was a rumble as the gate opened and the van lurched forward.

Grace tumbled on top of me.

'Sorry!' she mumbled.

The van drove forwards then rounded a corner and slowed to a halt. We waited for the sound of the driver getting out, then gently opened the back door. Archie peered out, looking to either side.

'Coast is clear,' he said.

We toppled out the back of the van and crouched down low, being careful in case there was anybody around that we hadn't seen. It looked like we were inside the loading bay.

'I think this is the area that leads off the storeroom hallway,' I said, imagining the gallery stacked above us from memory. 'I'd say the student artwork will be either by the door, waiting to be loaded, or sitting in the holding room, ready to go.'

The others nodded as we crept through the loading bay towards the back doors of the gallery.

There was a truck parked with its back right up to the doorway into the gallery. We couldn't tell if it was the truck picking up the artwork or not. But Margaret had said they were being picked up around lunchtime, so it could have been.

'We need to go inside and check the holding room,' I whispered, gesturing for the others to follow.

'Won't it be locked?' Sara asked.

I hoped not.

We snuck up to the back doors and saw they were propped open as a delivery man carried boxes out of the gallery and loaded them into his truck, before turning back to get more. While he was bending down, we funnelled past him into the gallery and ducked into the closest holding room, which was open.

'What do we do if we find Geoff?' I asked nervously.

'Just stay quiet. We'll deal with that if we come to it,' Sara said.

That didn't fill me with a lot of confidence. But I knew we had to get to the artwork to solve this mystery.

We began checking the packages and boxes spread

across the holding room.

'They're still here!' Grace called quietly, pointing to some packages that lined the walls. Sure enough, there was a stack of brown boxes, with the top one labelled 'Crestwood Hall'.

'Quick, find the one for Eden College!' I said excitedly.

We rifled through the packages, gently shifting the ones we'd checked to the other side of the room.

Suddenly Archie hissed, 'Found it!'

We all ran over to him as he pushed forward a box labelled 'Eden College'.

'Open it!' I said.

It was hard work, because the package was taped securely shut, but after a short amount of time, we managed to tear it open. Inside were all twelve works from Eden College.

'Now, let's find Grace's,' I instructed.

Grace saw the edge of her frame and pulled out her piece. 'Here it is!'

'Bring it over here,' I said breathlessly.

We brought Grace's artwork over to a metal table that stood in the corner of the room.

'Now, if I'm right . . .' I said. I could see Archie, Sara and Grace hold their breath.

I gently turned Grace's artwork over and slid the catches on the back of the frame. The frame loosened and I gently held the artwork in place as I turned it back over, so Grace's artwork was facing up. I lifted first the frame, then the glass and placed them to the side. Then I lifted Grace's painting up off the back of the frame. There was something behind it.

'Is that . . .' Archie began.

'You were right . . .' Grace whispered.

'No way . . .' Sara trailed off.

I placed Grace's painting carefully to the side and stood back.

There, sitting on the table, was the 16-million-dollar missing artwork, *The Holy Cherubim.*

Chapter 16

Even though I had explained to my friends back at the markets, they were shocked to see that my theory was actually correct.

'I can't believe you figured it out,' Grace whispered, as she stared at the valuable artwork.

'I worked it out when we realised the frame had changed. Why would someone steal Grace's artwork and then change the frame? To fit the hidden artwork! And Margaret had said the artworks are all micro-chipped—*The Holy Cherubim* should have sounded the alarms when it left the building. But it didn't.

Because maybe it *never left* the building. Maybe the thief was hiding the artwork until they could get it out of the gallery without being noticed. That's when it clicked. What better way to get the artwork out than to smuggle it out in a painting that people aren't watching? That policeman laughed at us about Grace's artwork being missing. He didn't care. They wouldn't even notice a *student's* artwork walking out the back door.'

'We must be right about it being an inside job,' Sara added. 'Only someone working here would know all this stuff. About the microchips. The loading bay. The time the student art was leaving and where it was going. It's the perfect crime.'

'And who better to know this stuff than a security guard?' Archie added. 'Geoff would have had all this information.'

'So, what do we do now?' Grace asked.

'We call the police and take this back up to the gallery,' I said firmly.

'There's no service down here,' Archie said, holding up his phone.

'Let's just take it up to the gallery, then,' Sara said.

'Not so fast!' a voice said from behind us, startling us all. We whipped around to see a person standing in the doorway, a grimace on their face.

But it wasn't Geoff.

'Margaret?' I asked, shaking my head in confusion.

'I heard what you said just now,' Margaret said, slowly stalking into the room. 'You are very clever, Ella. In fact, I can't believe you worked it all out. But there's one thing you didn't get right . . . Geoff had nothing to do with this.'

Margaret's usually kind face looked completely different. Her smile was gone, and in its place was a sinister sneer.

'It was . . . it was *you?!'* Archie gasped.

'That's right,' she laughed mockingly. 'You never suspected an old lady, did you?'

'I thought you were our friend,' I spluttered.

'Ha!' Margaret scoffed. 'Nobody cares about me. I'm just a lowly gallery assistant. But that's the thing, isn't it? Nobody would ever think I had the brains to carry out a multimillion-dollar art heist. But you kids just had to try and ruin everything, didn't you?'

'Margaret, don't do this,' Sara pleaded. 'Give the painting back and you might not get into too much trouble!'

Margaret laughed again. 'You kids have no idea. This painting is going to get me out of here. I won't need to work anymore. I can retire and live a life of luxury once I sell this. In fact, I have a buyer all lined up in Australia. And I was going to get it there, hidden safely away in your artwork, Grace. All they had to do was pick up your art shipment when it arrived in the country. Nobody would go looking for a silly child's missing art. They'd think it just got lost in transit. But you've wrecked that plan now, haven't you?'

'See? It's too late. The cat's out of the bag,' I said, trying to hide the waver in my voice. 'It's time to come clean.'

'You're right that the plan to send the painting to Australia in Grace's artwork has been ruined. But that won't stop me from taking *The Holy Cherubim* right now,' Margaret said, stepping forward. 'Hand it over! I'm stronger than I look.' She clenched her fists.

'We can take you on,' Grace said, standing in front of me and the painting. 'There's four of us. And only one of you!'

'Oh, but you see,' Margaret said menacingly. 'I have help.'

A large figure appeared in the doorway behind her. It was the security guard that had stopped us at the gallery entrance earlier.

'What do you want me to do with them, boss?' he said to Margaret.

'Never mind them, just get the artwork!' Margaret spat.

The security guard strode forward, his menacing form casting a shadow over us all. We stepped out of the way, leaving the artwork on the table. We all knew that we wouldn't be able to take on a fully grown security guard who also happened to look like a body builder.

The guard snatched up the painting.

'Gently, now!' Margaret hissed. 'That painting is

worth more than your life!'

The guard sneered. 'So, what do we do with these little meddlers?' he said, nodding in our direction.

I heard Sara whimper. Grace clasped my hand.

'We'll leave them here,' Margaret said. 'By the time they are found, we'll be long gone.'

Margaret turned to walk out the door.

'Margaret, don't do this!' I yelled after her.

She didn't look back, just strode out the doorway before the guard, who pressed a button on the other side. The electronic door whooshed shut. Then we heard a quiet *beep* and the sound of a lock engaging, trapping us in the holding room.

Grace ran to the door and tried to open it. It was shut tight. She hammered on the door.

'Help! Somebody, help!'

We tried our phones again, but there was still no service.

'Have you girls got a bobby pin?' Archie asked desperately. 'That's how they pick locks in the movies.'

Sara rolled her eyes. 'The lock is engaged with a

swipe card, not a key,' she said. 'And contrary to the movies, not all girls have bobby pins in their hair.'

Archie shrugged.

'There's gotta be a way out of here,' Grace said, looking around.

There were no windows in the holding room and no emergency exits. We even looked up at the ceiling, hoping for a manhole or air conditioning vent we could climb into.

Nothing.

'We've got to hurry,' I said desperately. 'Margaret is getting away with *The Holy Cherubim*.'

But it was no use. Even though we'd solved the mystery and found the thief, we couldn't figure out a way out of the holding room.

We were trapped. And nobody knew we were here.

Chapter 17

'We can't give up!' Archie said, standing up tall. 'Ella, you solved the mystery. Now it's up to us to get out of here and save the painting.'

'But how?' I asked mournfully.

'Let's search the room,' Archie said. 'It's a *storeroom*. There's got to be something in here that can help us. Something we can use to make a loud noise to attract attention. Or smash down the door. Anything!'

Sara and I exchanged hopeless glances.

But Grace's face brightened. 'Archie's right. It's not time to give up yet!'

We each went to a corner and began fossicking through the contents of the room. We opened boxes and cupboards and pulled things out, holding them up for each other to see in case anything sparked a brainwave.

There were cleaning supplies, artwork from the student exhibit, boxes of material for displays. Old frames. New frames. Mops and buckets. Grace tried to bang a mop against one of the buckets, but it only made a dull clunking sound.

'Hang on, what's this?' Archie said, opening a box.

We all gathered around him. Inside were pieces of tech equipment, from broken security cameras to old walkie-talkies.

'A walkie-talkie!' Sara said excitedly. She pulled it out of the box and flicked the switch on.

Nothing happened.

She flipped it over and loosened the battery compartment. It opened, but we were instantly disappointed to see it was empty.

'We need to find batteries! Pull out anything electronic,' I instructed.

I dug through the supplies in my corner of the room, but nothing took a battery.

After a couple of minutes of frantic digging, Grace shrieked, 'Here!' She held up a string of lights that was probably used to decorate exhibits. And instead of a plug, the lights were connected to a small battery pack.

We all held our breath as Grace jimmied open the pack. Inside sat four large batteries.

'Try them!' I screamed in excitement.

Grace pulled out the batteries and clicked them into the walkie-talkie. They were the right size.

'The moment of truth,' she said, looking up at us with hopeful eyes.

Grace flicked the switch on the walkie-talkie and it crackled to life.

'It worked!' she yelled. 'Hello? Hello? Is anyone there? Art gallery security? Geoff?!'

The walkie-talkie crackled some more, but there was no response.

'Help us! We're trapped in the holding room and we know where *The Holy Cherubim* is!'

We waited.

Nothing.

Suddenly, a crackly voice came across the speaker. 'Who is this?'

'Hello! Please help us! We're trapped,' Grace said desperately.

'Is this . . . is this the kids from Eden College and Crestwood Hall?' the voice said.

We knew that voice. It was Geoff!

'Geoff! It's us! Ella, Archie, Sara and Grace,' I said, grabbing the walkie-talkie.

'Where are you?!' he asked.

'In the storeroom by the loading bay. Margaret locked us in here. She has *The Holy Cherubim*!'

There was silence on the other end. The battery light on the walkie-talkie flickered.

'Hello?' I yelled.

Then the walkie-talkie went dead.

'Did he hear us?' Sara asked desperately.

Archie jumped up and began digging through the boxes and cupboards again, looking for more batteries.

I waited, my eyes focused on the locked door.

Suddenly, there was a *beep* and the door swung open.

It was Geoff! And he had two police officers with him.

'Are you kids OK?' he asked.

We ran to him, and he pulled us into a group hug.

'I couldn't hear properly on the walkie-talkie—it sounded like you said Margaret had stolen the painting!' he laughed.

'She did!' we yelled in unison.

Geoff looked shocked. The police looked confused.

'There's no time—we have to find her!' Archie said.

'I saw Margaret and one of the security guards, Peter, leaving the gallery on the security footage,' Geoff said. 'I thought it was a bit odd, but figured they had to go somewhere. They were carrying a package.'

'The Holy Cherubim!' Sara yelled.

'They got into Margaret's car—it's a red mini,' Geoff said.

The police jumped into action and began talking hurriedly into their own walkie-talkies. Moments later, the sound of blaring sirens could be heard.

'I don't understand how you worked it all out,' Geoff said, leading us back up to the main gallery.

'It was Ella,' Archie said proudly.

My cheeks flushed pink.

Geoff took us into the gallery office, where he gave us each some water. It was only now that we had escaped the holding room that the magnitude of what had happened began to sink in. I felt a little shaky. Geoff called the café and had them deliver some steaming banana bread, which we gobbled up thankfully.

Someone at the gallery called Crestwood Hall to tell them where we were and reassure them we were all safe and sound.

Geoff's phone buzzed and he stepped outside the office to take the call.

We sat waiting for the school staff to come and collect us.

'Do you think we'll be in trouble?' Grace asked.

'We did solve an international mystery that the police couldn't even crack,' I said. 'Surely that counts for something.'

'But we didn't catch her,' Sara said. 'Margaret is gone.'

Geoff stepped back into the office with a beaming smile. 'They got them!' he declared.

I looked at my friends with wide eyes.

'The police tracked Margaret's car and found her travelling towards the border. Peter was in the car with her, along with one other very precious item, hidden under the back seat.'

'The Holy Cherubim!' Archie cried.

Geoff nodded. 'I don't know how you did it. But you kids belong in Scotland Yard.'

My heart felt like it was expanding in my chest. I couldn't believe it! We'd saved a 16-million-dollar painting and solved a real-life London mystery! But as I looked around the room, I realised that wasn't the best thing I'd found on this international adventure. Grace squeezed my hand, as Sara winked at me and Archie smiled. Even on the other side of the world, there was still one thing better than anything else.

New friends.

Chapter 18

'Intelligence. Bravery. Teamwork. That's what we've witnessed amongst these young people. But what I love the most is that these students have come together from across the globe and forged a true friendship. A friendship that looks out for each other. A friendship that cares. And this is something the entire world can learn from.'

The Crestwood Great Hall, full of students, parents and teachers, as well as journalists and photographers, broke into applause.

The Mayor of London cleared his throat and spoke

again. 'Ella, Grace, Archie and Sara. Please come up on the stage.'

My legs felt shaky as I walked up the steps to the podium. I looked out into the audience and could see Mrs Hodges and our friend, Geoff, sitting in the front row, smiling at us. I climbed the final step onto the stage and stood in front of the mayor with my friends.

He gestured for us to step forward, and, one by one, he hung a medal around our necks. 'This is in honour of your bravery,' he said, smiling.

Down the front, photographers from different newspapers snapped our photos as the mayor shook each of our hands. Across their heads, I locked eyes with Geoff. He clapped his hands above his head and nodded. I beamed back at him.

When the presentation was finished and the mayor had left, Mrs Hodges came over and hugged me and Grace tightly. Grace gave me a funny look. Hugging a teacher was not cool.

'I'm so proud of you four,' she said, also nodding at Archie and Sara. 'I mean, what you did was dangerous and I hope you've learnt that you need to come to an adult if there's ever something serious like that going on again.'

We nodded solemnly (which means very seriously), even though I secretly knew we wouldn't do anything different if we had the chance again.

'But I'm so proud of how brave and clever you all were,' Mrs Hodges said, beaming. 'And just think, this will be the *third* time you've been in the London papers in one trip!'

Grace blushed, remembering her incident at the Trafalgar Square fountain.

Then we all burst out laughing.

'Well, we may not have met the Queen, but getting a medal from the Mayor of London is pretty special,' I said, laughing lightly.

Despite my happiness, I felt a lump of sadness sitting in my throat.

'So, this is it,' Sara said.

Grace and I looked at each other. We both had tears in our eyes. It was time to board the bus for the airport and leave Crestwood Hall for good.

Sara leaned forward and pulled Grace into a tight hug. And then she moved along and hugged me tightly, too. 'Make sure you email me,' she said.

Archie stepped forward shyly. 'Great to know you, Grace,' he said, giving her a quick hug. Then Archie moved over to me. 'And you too, Ella,' he said, his cheeks colouring pink. 'You're such a smart girl.' His voice sounded nervous and shaky.

My own cheeks flushed, and Sara nudged Grace and giggled slightly.

Archie leant forward and hugged me. 'I'll miss you, Ella,' he whispered.

We pulled apart right as Mrs Hodges came bustling through the crowd of Eden girls, who were all tearfully saying goodbye to their new friends.

'Come on then, girls, onto the bus!' she said.

We said our final farewells and walked over to the bus, climbing up the steps and taking our seats. I looked out the bus window as the engine choked to life. The Crestwood Hall students stood waving at the entrance to the school. I could even see Kai, standing next to Archie with a kind hand upon his shoulder.

We all waved, as the bus chugged up the road until Crestwood Hall was nothing but a small speck in the distance behind us.

'I can't believe we're going home,' Grace said. 'The trip seems like it went by in a flash, but it also feels like we were here for years.'

'I know what you mean,' I said, dabbing my tears with a tissue. 'But we've got a whole lot of memories that I don't think we'll ever forget.'

Grace pulled out her phone. 'One last photo?' she said.

I leaned in as she positioned the camera in front of us.

'Say "London"!' she laughed. And gently clicked the button.

× –

From: Ella

Sent: Wednesday, 7:42 PM (UTC+10:00) Sydney

To: Archie; Sara

Subject: G'day!

Hi Archie and Sara,

I should say g'day, because we are back in Australia! The flight was soooo long. But it's good to be home. Everyone couldn't believe our story of how we caught the art thief of London. It even made the newspapers back here! And my story explaining how we solved the case of the missing multimillion-dollar painting was one of the most clicked-on stories Eden Press has ever published! (It probably helped that the headline sounded just like a *Millie Mysteries*!)

I heard Margaret and Peter were sentenced to prison for stealing. Even though I know she wasn't a true friend, I still feel sad for Margaret.

I've been through all my photos of our adventures in London and I've created a whole poster collage to hang on my wall. I've attached my favourite one to this email.

I hope you like it!

Don't forget to keep in touch. I miss you both.

Love always, Ella

x